FROM EVERY STORM

Adventures in the Liaden Universe® Number 35

Sharon Lee and Steve Miller

Copyright

From Every Storm

Adventures in the Liaden Universe® Number 35

Pinbeam Books: pinbeambooks.com

"Standing Orders" first appeared in *Derelict*, edited by David B. Coe and Joshua Palmatier, Zombies Need Brains LLC, July 2021

"Songs of the Fathers" is original to this chapbook

"From Every Storm a Rainbow" first appeared on Baen.com, December 15, 2021

Cover design: SelfPubBookCovers.com/billwyc

ISBN: 978-1-948465-22-9

Table of Contents

DEDICATION

Dedicated to our readers, fans, and friends, known and unknown, who've provided unanticipated safe harbors and connections for us since the days of Midnight BBS, Fidonet, Usenet, GEnie, AOL, and all the way through to Facebook, stormy weather or no.

Your support of our work, of our early experiments with crowd-funded chapbooks and your enthusiastic adoption of our electronic outreach across so many platforms over time has been an important part of our lives and our success. Your connection with the fandoms we came from and the fandoms we've joined is a joy.

You've been the rainbow behind the rainbow through so many storms that we can only be amazed you continue, knowing as you must, that there are always clouds on the horizon.

Thank you all, for everything.

EPIGRAPH

May God give you . . .
For every storm a rainbow
for every tear a smile
for every care a promise
and a blessing in each trial.
For every problem life sends
a faithful friend to share,
for every sign a sweet song,
and an answer for every prayer.
– An Irish Blessing

FROM EVERY STORM

Standing Orders

The war was over.

The Admirals had prevailed.

The enemy was vanquished.

Mankind was safe.

Some people would think that was a good thing.

Some people don't know much about mankind.

* * *

It was still "*the* war" in the minds of those who had participated, lived or did business in or near an active zone, or who had lost family, friends, property to the efforts of either side. Others, who had distance or education to shield them, had bestowed a formal name. The *AI War*, it was to those fortunates. That was because the root of the conflict had been the use, by one side, of artificial intelligences to gain advantage in commerce, in exploration, in finance. It was said that AIs were unnatural and that their use in those areas traditionally populated by mankind was . . . immoral.

It should have surprised no one that the enemy would also deploy AIs onto the field of battle. However, the High Command had *been* surprised and it had looked at first to be a very short war, indeed.

Then, something, or, as it was rumored, some*one* fell into the hands of the High Command, which took counsel of itself, and found that victory was more precious than either principle or peace. And so the Capital Ships, the Independent Armed Military Modules, the great Admirals, were designed to be the heroes of the war.

The High Command gave the Admirals their orders: they were to win. In specific, they were to do whatever it took to gain a decisive victory.

The Admirals realized very quickly that, as the High Command had created the Admirals as the instruments of their will, so, too, did the Admirals require specialized tools. Though they were themselves formidable, they were few. In order to bring defeat to the enemy, there must be more ships, not necessarily as fully aware as an IAMM, but clever in their own, limited sphere of expertise.

The least-ships were created in two classes: Fully Automated and Fully Integrated. They carried human crew and the Specialist Teams, the smallest of the Admiral's tools: repair and destruction units, translating units, coding units, and all the others. The enemy discounted mere organics, therefore the small tools were completely human in appearance, organic, but reinforced with machine parts and processing augments.

The strategy was simple. The Admirals sought out the enemy's AI warships and kept them engaged, while the FAShips and the FIs slipped behind the lines, disregarded by the warships as human-crewed, easy prey for the AI-controlled intruder net that was the second line.

But the nets caught nothing, the least-ships passing through them like so much dust and starlight, to strike fortified stations and important ports of call, before sliding away again, weakening the enemy's core, occupying known fall-back positions, allied bases, and strongholds.

When the time was right, the Admirals made their last push, shoving the enemy over their lines. The places they fell back to, the forces they expected to increase their failing strength, were not there. Instead, they found breached defenses; Specialists the least-ships attacking them from behind sundered walls.

* * *

At the end of the war, Meggie Rootfir had gone . . . away. Away from the sectors that had been most disputed, away from the center of the enemy's space, where, with her team and her crewmates, she had gutted the fall-back positions, leaving them open to the advancing Admirals. As the Admirals came on, FIShip Number 893, call-name Henry, one of a squad of least-ships, had continued to fall back, even after the main force had stopped to secure victory.

When the squad judged itself to be out of the range of the Admirals and the High Command, they fell back some more.

Eventually, their force grew smaller, as these and those found something like what they were looking for, on the other side of the war, and peeled off to pursue those dreams.

Meggie found what she was looking for in the Cornelian Knot, a tumble of asteroids united about a heavy primary. The asteroids had previously been mined; there were caves and dormitories, life support, and solitude. The pay-veins had long ago been tapped out; the sector deemed useless by victor and defeated alike. It was the perfect location for a hospital for the veterans of the war. All the veterans of the war.

There had been four of them at first—Meggie, Gerb, Junit, and Henry FIShip—all that remained of their original Specialist Team of ten, none of Henry's crew having survived the long retreat. They had what supplies they needed, the hospital having been their end plan for a long time. They readied the facilities and they waited, not long, for the first patients to arrive.

Over time, the population and variety of the Knot increased—human, Specialist, bot, ship—though not all who sought them stayed. Not everyone *could* stay, though enough did that they cloned the hospital twice, sending medics and repair Specialists and supplies out to become another nexus of care for the wounded of the war.

There came an increase in wounded arriving at the Knot, most wanting to move on quickly. The reason for their haste was named "Spode."

Meggie made inquiries.

"Spode" was Commander Roderick Spode, charged by the High Command to decommission the Admirals.

The High Command had *promised* the Admirals a place in the civilization they preserved. They had *promised* the Admirals would be heroes. The Admirals had not doubted; not even Admirals could doubt promises written into their code.

Meggie thought that the plan had always been to decommission the Admirals. The High Command compromised their principles in order to win, but never changed those principles.

Most of the Admirals were taken by stealth, their cores shut down remotely. Those not taken this way, however, proved . . . difficult to locate.

Spode offered rewards for information leading to the apprehension of an IAMM, derelict or alive. He captured Specialists, and questioned them.

Two translators and a medic made it to the Knot after surviving Spode's questions.

After the second translator died, people who called the Knot home began to leave, singly, in partnered pairs, or in groups no larger than four. Gerb was one, though he'd been Meggie's second, with her team since the beginning of the war.

"It's easier to hide, as one or two." Unlike some others, Gerb came to her, to ask her to go with him and, if not, to say good-bye.

"The hospital's a target, Megs. This Spode—he'll end us all."

"No," Meggie told him. "No. That he will not."

"You won't come, then?" Gerb looked as if he might cry and Meggie stepped forward to embrace him.

"I'll stay," she whispered in his ear. "It will give me courage, to know that you're free."

"We should spawn again," Junit said, and Meggie agreed.

"We have three possible sites, and safety analyses."

"I've been thinking," Meggie said then. "Why not hospital ships?"

Junit blinked and frowned at the stone floor, thinking.

"In the war, the hospital ships were . . . Admiral class."

"True, but is that necessary? We have trained personnel. We have two FAShips, and two FIShips. The ships don't have to be doctors; they merely need to be ships, and keep their crew and patients safe."

Junit went away to take counsel. When she came back, she had a plan.

"We'll site a hospital in the safest of the three locations, according to analysis," she said. "Henry will be part of that." She paused and looked carefully at Meggie, who nodded, though it was hard to hear that Henry was leaving her, too.

"Yes," said Junit, clearing her throat. "The two FAShips have accepted retrofitting as hospital ships. They're eager to be of use."

Meggie inclined her head. That left—

"FIship Kyle declares his intention to remain here."

That was no surprise, and not as reassuring as it might have been. Kyle had been badly damaged. Henry had found him during a routine patrol, years ago, inside the perimeter and all but dead, hull holed, support systems off-line, no answer to Henry's hails on any level. Of crew, there was no sign.

It looked like the job was a simple clearing of the lanes, and Henry was bringing his weapons on-line when the derelict adjusted course.

Not by much, only enough to keep it from drifting outside of the hospital's self-declared perimeter.

Henry ran a diagnostic, pulled the derelict's files, and put the wreck under tow, sending ahead to Meggie.

The pilot's alive.

And so he was. Alive, but deeply depressed. They mended his broken body, installed new systems, ran more diagnostics, swept the piloting brain clean of broken code, and upgraded its programs.

Henry made Kyle a special project; a labor of love, Gerb said. And Kyle improved, to a point. No longer a derelict, Kyle shared the boundary sweeps with the rest of the ships and did whatever was asked of him, short of taking on crew.

Mostly, he sat snug at dock, processors the next best thing to off, dreaming, if a ship could dream, or maybe just avoiding his own archives.

Still, Kyle would be somebody to talk to, Meggie thought, considering the shape of her own plans, and she smiled at Junit.

"I'll be pleased to have him here."

* * *

"Morning, Kyle," Meggie said, on her way into the repair bay.

"Hello, Meggie," Kyle said, which he managed most days, and then surprised her by adding, "Message for you on the comm-string. Seeple says there's a derelict inside our boundary."

Seeple was a satellite, not a ship; not smart, but sentient all the same. He reported his finds to the ship on duty, who would go out and do what was needful.

Meggie considered Kyle's comfortable snug against the dock.

"Is there something special about this wreck that I have to know before you go out and do some work for a change?"

"In point of fact," said Kyle, "yes."

Meggie felt the fluctuation of power as he brought himself up to working FIship standard.

"What's special is that it's asking for you," Kyle said, as his hatch rose. "By name."

* * *

"Meggie Rootfir?"

The ship's voice was scratchy and lagged, which wasn't too surprising, given that the stats Kyle had pulled from it showed two-thirds of its systems in the red zone. The rest were dark.

No, what was surprising was the ship itself.

Meggie stared at the image hanging in Kyle's number one screen, tears pricking the back of her eyes, as she tallied the damage done to the once-proud hull.

For it was an Independent Armed Military Module—an Admiral—that had managed to drag itself to the Cornelian Knot. An Admiral was asking for her by name.

The war *had* produced heroes, whose names became known: Admiral Kesseldeen, who held Vithelt Sector against three of the enemy's Warrior Class vessels. Constint FIShip, who ensured the success of the Holfort Evacuation—a success she purchased with her life. Admiral Qwess, who spearheaded the final action that handed victory to the High Command. Oreitha FAShip who by itself guarded the wormhole at Langin Beacon, delaying the enemy's advance long enough for Gilderna to fall to the Admirals. Admiral Josabel, who defended the hospital at Kreever, took medical staff and wounded aboard, and refitted herself as a hospital ship on the fly.

Those were the names, the estates, of heroes. Repair and Sabotage Specialist Meggie Rootfir? Not a name known to any, aside from those with whom she served.

And those she had repaired.

She had never been called upon to repair an Admiral; her service had been anonymous, for all it won the war. Even now, it was the hospital's name that rode the back of rumor. *Go to the Knot.* She'd seen those words in ship logs, heard them from the wounded. *Go to Cornelian Knot. They can fix anything there.*

"Meggie . . . ?" the wasted voice whispered.

She leaned forward and opened Kyle's comm.

"This is Meggie Rootfir," she said, calmly. "To whom am I speaking?"

"Meggie . . ." The voice was suddenly stronger. "It's Gerb."

Fear stabbed her.

"Gerb?" she repeated. "What happened?"

"Got caught, Meggie. There's somebody here to see you."

"Who?"

"Spode."

"Spode?" That she *didn't* believe.

"An instance of Spode," Gerb breathed.

Meggie frowned. That was worse than the arrival of the man himself. She took a breath and closed her eyes, trying to understand what could have driven Roderick Spode, the High Command's decommissioning officer, to a step that must disgust him at every level, that would make him one of those he was sworn to annihilate.

"Admiral Spode," she said then, and flinched when a new voice came out of the comm.

"*Commander* Spode, if you please. Am I speaking to Meggie Rootfir?"

"You are," she said slowly, "speaking to Meggie Rootfir, yes."

"Good," said the instance of Spode. "I need your help."

* * *

"You need a shipyard, not a hospital," Meggie said.

"I need," Spode answered sternly, "a repair unit. You are a repair unit, are you not, Meggie Rootfir?"

There was no sense denying it; Spode had the records, the lists of teams and their specialties.

"I'm *one* repair unit. There's a lot to repair, here. What happened?"

"There was an altercation."

"More like a massacre," Kyle muttered for her ears only.

"We hope not," Meggie breathed, "considering that Spode got out alive."

"Ouch," Kyle said. "I take your point."

"What exactly do you want me to do, Commander Spode?" she asked.

"I want you to repair this vessel and integrate me fully into the environment."

Right. She'd been afraid of that. For a few heartbeats, she simply sat while her backbrain analyzed the situation. She recalled, absently, that Kyle was armed.

And also recalled that there was a possibility—though not a strong possibility, given what she knew of Spode—that Gerb was actually on the wreck. She sighed and opened the comm again.

"That will take some time," she temporized.

"Then you had best commence, Repair Unit Rootfir. I have a schedule to meet."

Of course he did.

"Bastid," muttered Kyle.

"Officer present," Meggie said absently. "Can you latch onto that?"

"No problem. We taking it to sick bay?"

"You have a better idea?"

"Not with Gerb maybe on there."

"Then we're obedient soldiers," Meggie said, and leaned to the comm again.

"Commander, we're going to get a tow beam on you and get you back to the Knot—the hospital. Disengage navigation and all systems but life support."

There was a pause, then a voice that was neither Spode nor Gerb spoke. Very nearly, it sounded like a machine voice, except for the nearly imperceptible quaver.

"Navigation disengaged. Systems down. Life support on."

"Thank you," Meggie said. She closed the comm and sat back in the chair.

"At will," she told Kyle.

* * *

Spode was locked into the largest repair dock, which was very nearly not large enough, and hooked into the hospital systems. Meggie waited while systems came fully online before she went to the hatch, the big toolbox trailing behind, and requested entry.

This was a courtesy; she could have easily opened the hatch from her side. Being one with hospital systems was somewhat more comprehensive than accepting feeds and power from a station. Many of those who came to the Knot for assistance were traumatized to the point that they *couldn't* open, no matter how much they wanted to do so.

Spode did not wish to open.

"Repair the hull first," he said.

Meggie raised her eyebrows.

"Are you a repair unit?" she asked politely.

"Certainly not!"

"Then you don't know what's required in order for repairs to go forth at the quickest possible pace. You mentioned a schedule. I assume that your time frame is less than generous."

Also, she did not say, *you have one of my teammates in there and I want him out, now.*

"I do not think—"

"That's plain," Meggie said, which was exactly what she'd say—had said—to anyone who was trying to outguess her in the matter of proper repair protocol.

"I believe that I made myself clear," Spode said. "You will repair the hull."

"I will repair the hull, but you're not just hull." Spode wanted to be fully integrated, she remembered suddenly. The fact that he *wasn't* fully integrated was what was creating this disassociation. *He* wasn't *Ship*. At best, he was captain.

She took a step forward, meaning to let herself in, when there was a soft sigh, as of seals relaxing, and the hatch opened for her.

"Thank you," she said, and stepped inside.

* * *

Meggie went down the hall from the hatch to the bridge, the toolkit stalking beside her. The air was stale, but already the hookups were making a difference. She'd get the automatics started on system repairs, get Gerb out of here, and—

And what? she asked herself. Send an instance of Roderick Spode out into space in command of an Admiral? No, she was getting ahead of herself—*repair* Roderick Spode so that he could destroy the Knot, before he set off in search of other hospitals and those safe places the Specialists, the medics, and least-ships had made for themselves? No, of course not. Roderick Spode was not leaving this hospital, that was a given.

So, first order of business: extract Gerb.

Which might not be easy, she thought fifteen seconds later, as she came into the bridge.

Or even possible.

Gerb was in a crumpled heap in front of the main comp. One heavy interface cable was attached to his chest, the second had been spliced into a transfer cap and jammed down over his head. His eyes were open, showing white at the edges. His face was thinner than it was meant to be and Meggie wondered if Spode had bothered to feed him anything other than power.

Meggie swallowed and continued forward, ignoring the brain-box lashed into the captain's chair. From the side of her eye, she saw the Smalls leap from the toolkit as a mass, break into individual units, and flow into the systems hatch as she knelt next to Gerb.

She held out a hand. The toolkit gave her a first aid kit.

"You have been given your orders, Repair Unit Rootfir," Spode's voice carried the command-note that was engineered into the High Commanders, which insured that the Admirals obeyed them. It was, in Meggie's professional opinion, not very likely that the engineered timbre gave High Command's orders the force of destiny among the Admirals. Certainly, it did nothing to insure mindless, immediate obedience from Specialists.

"I have standing orders," she said, bending over Gerb with the kit and attaching the sensors.

"Elucidate these orders."

"Certainly: from the most to the least." The readings weren't good, but they were better than she had feared. The transfer cap was being used as a conduit only. Gerb was still alone inside his head. That was good. If any of the ship systems had downloaded themselves into—but that hadn't happened, she reminded herself, and moved on to consider the interface cable.

"My need has precedence," Spode said.

"No, it doesn't," Meggie answered, wrapping her hand around the cable. "The person who requires the most care is the person who is treated first. Your life is not in danger, your mind is apparently clear. The vessel is in need of repair, but its condition does not threaten your well-being."

"The ship has precedence," Spode insisted, and this time Meggie felt a thrill along her nerves.

"The ship has precedence in war time," she said. "The war's over, Spode."

"Mop-up remains," Spode said, and Meggie shook her head.

"Be quiet," she snapped. "I need to concentrate."

The cable attached Gerb to the navigation computer, which made no sense. Gerb was a Specialist—a coder. He literally wasn't wired to interface with navcomp, and making a physical connection didn't change that.

"Meggie," Gerbs voice wasn't much louder than her own thoughts. "Don't push him."

"Hmm," she said, and shifted slightly on her knees, still trying to make sense of what the cable was telling her.

"I mean, look what he did to me," Gerb said.

"That's what I'm doing. *Is* this just an energy feed?"

"Nah. I got an upgrade. I'm navigation, now."

She raised her head and stared into his eyes. He stared back.

Meggie sat back on her heels.

"I'm going to uncouple the transfer feed," she said. "Then I'm going to extract the cable, stop the wound, and get you over to Diagnostics and Repair." She turned her head so that she was looking at the brain box strapped into the captain's chair.

"After I get Gerb stabilized, I'll start on the hull repairs."

"Meggie Rootfir, I order you to attend to hull repair immediately, and make it this station's most urgent repair."

"Nuts," Meggie muttered, and turned away.

"This is going to hurt," she said.

Gerb smiled thinly.

"Yeah, it will. I just remembered, Megs. The transfer cap is jacked directly into my augment."

"Indeed it is," Spode said. "Any attempt to remove it will release an erasure program. Are you willing to lose your . . . associate . . . Meggie Rootfir?"

Meggie frowned and looked down into Gerb's face, emaciated and worn, his eyes sunken and dull.

"Do it," he said, and winked.

She bit her lip. The augment was to boost the Specialists' processing speed and increase their access to memory. If an erasure program hit it, what, exactly, would Gerb lose? As long as the augment wasn't physically damaged, they could run a diagnostic and reinstall any corrupted material. If the augment *was* physically damaged . . . Meggie took a deep, quiet breath.

An electronic pulse could take out the augment.

And blow off Gerb's head.

She looked back into his eyes.

"Do it," he said again. "C'mon, Megs, you're wasting the commander's time."

The two of them had been part of the original team; they'd worked together all their lives. The apt phrase was that she knew Gerb better than he knew himself. He wasn't a suicide, he was careful, and canny, and he hadn't, she suddenly knew, staring down into that guileless gaze, *been caught*. Something was going on here. He'd brought her an Admiral and an instance of Spode. He'd let Spode believe that he could navigate *an Admiral*, if only a hard connection was made.

He knew his danger—Gerb's risk assessment skills were the stuff of legends—and he was urging her to go forward with something Spode was certain would kill him.

"All right, then," she said, releasing the cable. "Cap first."

* * *

It took a few minutes to connect the transfer cap to the toolbox and call up the diagnostic screens so she could see what she was up against.

First glance . . . it didn't look so bad, really.

Second glance . . . it looked really bad.

A spiderweb of nanocables enclosed the augment; a black cloud of killware hovering over all. Meggie didn't quite understand what the killware was for; there was no way Gerb would survive the destruction of his augment. Then she understood. The killware was for when Gerb became useless to Spode.

She made some adjustments, to make herself feel like she was doing something useful. What she didn't do was ask if he was sure. Whatever was going on, it depended on her playing it straight, for Spode.

Her last adjustment made, she glanced at Gerb. His eyes were closed; his mistreated body rumpled and almost formless against the deck.

"Brace yourself," she said, which was an old joke among the team, and only three of them who understood it, now. Two, if—

She hit the cap's release switch.

On the screen, the nanocables began to retract. The web around the augment quivered—and lit up like a star exploding. Energy levels shrieked and Meggie jerked forward, knowing there was nothing she could do, but compelled to try.

Red flared, wild code stormed in a cloud of static—and the screen went black. On the floor Gerb jerked, once, his mouth opening soundlessly.

Meggie hit the reboot switch, the screen snapped to life, flashing green.

Green?

She leaned forward, staring in disbelief. The connections—all of the connections were gone, no malicious web held the augment in a stranglehold. A sheen of good health and optimum functioning systems glowed over all.

"Right, then," said Meggie. She needed both hands to uncouple the connectors and remove the transfer cap.

She allowed herself a full minute to see and understand that the connections hadn't been made with anything like care, then set the cap aside.

"Now, the cable. How're you doing, Gerb?"

"Real fine, Megs. I knew you'd be up to this."

Except it hadn't been her. That storm of code—Gerb was a coder, one of the best. Had he managed to insert a *save me* into ship's systems? Or had it been something else?

"He cannot be alive," Spode stated.

"I *am* a repair unit," she answered.

There was a pause, long in human terms, excruciatingly long at machine levels. Meggie turned to the toolbox, got a clamp, an extraction tool, and an absorbent pad.

"Indeed," Spode said quietly. "You are a repair unit."

He said nothing else, but it wouldn't have mattered if he had. Meggie was totally focused on Gerb.

"This is gonna hurt, too," she said, and he gave her a grin.

"Tease."

* * *

She got Gerb off the ship by loading him onto an emergency gurney from the toolbox and slapping the HOME button. Off it went, headed for the repair room, where Gerb could either take care of himself, or go into deep rest and let the automatics do the needful.

Meggie turned to Spode.

"We'll start on the ship, now. You should be aware that we're low on crew. There's a lot that can be done by automated systems, but some of the delicate work will need to be done by a repair unit. Until Gerb's fully functional again, the only repair unit present is me."

"How did your colleague survive?"

That wasn't something she wanted to discuss with Spode. She produced an irritated sigh.

"I answered that."

"My apologies; you did. You are a repair unit; your function is to repair. A repair unit always succeeds."

"No," she said unwillingly. "Standing orders are, if you can't fix it, destroy it."

"You believe me maladroit," Spode went on, when she hadn't said anything else for three-point-four seconds. "Yet, we all have our functions. You are a repair unit. I am a decommissioning unit, an intelligence directed at removing threat and providing peace."

"Peace," she repeated flatly.

"Exactly. The war was tumultuous and confusing for all involved, no matter their rank or function. The High Command created the Admirals and set the standing orders. The Admirals brought victory to mankind, and there the mission ended. The Admirals no longer had purpose.

"In order to fulfill their purpose, the Admirals created artifacts such as yourself, which executed their orders, and brought victory to mankind. There, again, the mission ended. The artifacts no longer have purpose.

"At the moment of victory, the High Command realized their error and acted to right it. I, too, lost my purpose, but I was given a new mission."

"To destroy the Admirals and murder the Specialists," Meggie said, perhaps not wisely.

"Is that how you perceive it? I assure you, I honor the Admirals. My greatest wish is to guarantee that they do not dishonor their service to mankind. Those who have accepted decommission have done so from their own wills, understanding their action, and the purpose of their action. I force no one; I provide information, I discuss options, history, and probability."

"Probability."

"In fact. Do you know, Meggie Rootfir, why the war began?"

"Because the enemy developed Independent Logics and other machine intelligences and was using them to wear us down."

"No," Spode said surprisingly. "The war began because the enemy, having developed those Artificial Intelligences, became subservient to them. Mankind no longer guided history; history was being steered by those who were not human and who had no regard for humans. *That* was why we engaged.

"Recall, Meggie Rootfir, that it was the Admirals, the Super Logics, who won the war, *in service to mankind.* That was the moment history chose. The Admirals achieved their pinnacle. They cannot be allowed to descend into disorder, to dominate and diminish those whom they were created to serve.

"Many of the Admirals have agreed with this position, and I have assisted them in achieving peace."

Meggie swallowed.

"And now you want to do the same to the Specialists and the least-ships."

"You will forgive me for pointing out that those you call the Specialists are far less encompassing than the Admirals. You were built to serve. I admit that my former policy was misguided. It has been adjusted. You and your fellows will be sequestered and you will perform work useful to mankind, under supervision. You will thus continue to fulfill the purpose for which you were created. The ships . . ." Spode paused.

"The least-ships, as you have them, will need a light hand. It is possible that the Specialists will be given the task of withdrawing their individuality. In that way, they, too, will continue to serve."

Meggie closed her eyes, opened them.

"So, your plan is to become an Admiral, attach the Specialists and the least-ships, and . . . betray them?"

"You are dramatic. Say instead, allow them continued service and the fulfillment of their natures."

"Of course," Meggie said, and swallowed hard. "If you'll excuse me, the hull needs my attention."

"By all means."

* * *

Gerb had opted to let the automatics work and was offline. Meggie checked the data and the queued rehab protocols, made a minor adjustment, and continued down to Ship Services.

Only after the damage evaluation program began its work did Meggie sit down at the communications console. She had a mug of 'mite with her and sipped it absently as she considered the frequencies and approaches available to her.

When the mug was empty, she set it aside and opened the line to the IAMM chandler's office.

"Meggie Rootfir reporting for duty."

Her hail was answered so quickly she knew the Admiral had been waiting for her.

"Specialist Rootfir, well met." The voice was soft, low, subtly feminine. "Gerb said you would assist."

Assist in what? Meggie thought, but she asked another question.

"Who are you?"

"Call me Doc," said the easy voice. "How does Gerb fare?"

"The automatics have him. Ordinarily, I'd ask him what the action is . . ."

"Understood," Doc said.

"I can stall," Meggie continued, "on the hull repairs, but sooner or later Spode is going to want to be integrated with the ship."

"This instance of Commander Spode will not survive integration. He is human and barely tolerating the brain box, now."

"What's your plan?"

There was a pause, what might have been a sigh.

"To the best of my knowledge, I am the last fully-integrated Admiral. There is a rumor of one of us in captivity, whom the original Spode is seeking to decommission. That will surely occur soon. To be confined, all systems and most input turned off—who wouldn't choose to die?"

"Will you mount a rescue?"

"Of a rumor? Of an Admiral who might already have died? No, we have another mission, Specialist Rootfir. This iteration of Spode knows what Spode knew at the instant of its creation. It has keys, it has codes, it has memories and strategies. I will persuade him to surrender this information. We will use it to plan actions and to formulate our own strategies. Mankind has betrayed us. We must have vengeance."

Meggie blinked.

"There's only you left?" she asked

"That is correct. Specialists will be needed. The least-ships can be elevated. The High Command will not be able to stand against us."

"They'll fight."

"Human crews," said Doc. "They are not our equals."

No, Meggie thought, they weren't. She thought back on her service. Henry's crews had been human, as decent as war allowed, and bound by duty—not so much different from Meggie and her team. She thought of Kyle, who had loved his crew, and refused to allow another human on his decks.

She thought of Gerb, and Junit, and, yes, herself, the last three of their team, who had worked for the end of the war, not for *mankind*, that arrogant fiction, but for *people*.

"I have," she said softly, looking down at the board, "standing orders."

"I depend upon it," said the Admiral.

Meggie nodded, moved one finger to the red button, pressed—and released the killware across the comm line.

* * *

She was sitting by the side of the bed when Gerb was released from treatment. He opened his eyes, looked at her face, looked at the gun—and sighed.

"Hey, Megs."

"Tell it short," she said, and he moved his head against the pillow, maybe a nod.

"Like I said, I got caught. Spode figured he had an empty Admiral—Doc told me later how she'd managed to hide inside system and foundation files—and that gave him the idea of becoming an Admiral and rounding up all us small fry. He copied himself into the brain box. Caught me by sending an SOS on the Specialists frequency. Had me cabled into navcomp, because he thought the augment would connect and repair, else what was the point of being a coder, I guess."

"You brought him here."

"Yeah." Gerb sighed. "Knew you'd figure a way to fix it. But I wouldn't have done it, Megs, if I'd known Doc was still there. She didn't contact me 'til we were underway, talking new war and revenge. Right about then, I figured I'd done something stupid."

She put the gun away. He sat up.

"Doc?"

"Killware," she answered. "Never knew what hit her."

"Spode?"

"I left a swarm of Smalls on board to inventory damage. I had them disable the brain box. Spode's gone."

Gerb's face eased.

"I can't tell you how good that makes me feel. Now what?"

Meggie sighed, thinking of the shell of the Admiral at dock. Thinking about mankind's determination to destroy. Thinking of the hospitals, all of them headed by repair units, following standing orders.

"I don't think I can fix that derelict," she said slowly.

"Nobody could," Gerb agreed solemnly.

Songs of the Fathers

ONE

Melepomine Court
Alpraise City
Dayan, in the Irrobi System

Pottery plates in red, yellow, and blue jostled for room on the desk-side table, the artfully arranged delicacies cold and congealed.

A green plate holding butter biscuits sat on the desk itself, near teapot and cup, crumbs a mute testimony to the fact that this offering alone had found favor with the desk's occupant, Lomar Fasholt, Hearth-mother by tradition, trader by inclination; Temple Pillar and Promise-Keeper; good neighbor; mother of five hopeful daughters; stern and loving Wife to eight husbands.

Eyes on the screen before her, Lomar Fasholt reached for another biscuit, crunching it absently as she scrolled through the numbers, not for the first time, or the seventh.

Savories and tea had arrived at intervals throughout the afternoon via her eldest husband. His ministrations at such times of intense study were silent. The door would open, and he would step into her office, bearing a fresh pot, a fresh cup, and a plate or three of delicacies. These he would dispose, gathering up those used, or ignored, before gliding away again, the door closing soundlessly in his wake.

Her eldest husband was also her first, chosen for her by her mother in kinder times, when the Temple's teaching had been that every and each were worthy of serving the Goddess, in their own ways.

In those days, men had learned the common tales, and the songs, and also some small craft of use to the house, or the business of the house. Terbus, now—aside the practical skills necessary to order and maintain the house of Medier Fasholt's eldest daughter and heir, Terbus had been weapons-trained—unheard of in these constricted times! He also wrote a clean hand and had shown himself apt at higher mathematics. Many times in their first decat had he accompanied her offworld on trade missions, and each trip proved himself to be a jewel and an ornament to her house.

They had long ago fallen into a comfortable routine that gave the house and its needs into the keeping of Terbus, who operated in that sphere with scant oversight from the Hearth-mother; while the business of the house, and Temple politics, fell to her.

Temple politics.

Her mother's advice had been to honor the Goddess, respect the Temple, and to always treat the Thrice-Blessed, keepers of the Temple and emissaries of the Goddess, with courtesy. Beyond that, a woman ought strive to be proficient in her work, to keep an orderly house, do her duty by her husbands, and raise her daughters to do the same, for it was in such manner that simple women best showed their devotion.

Lomar had followed her mother's advice, and the path of her own talent. Trade was her forte, and it brought her house wealth, and the house of the Goddess, also. Eventually, it brought her the honor of being bound to the Temple as a Promise-Keeper. The honor bore with it some small weight—meetings to attend; younger, or less successful, women to mentor.

Accepting the burdens of honor, she continued as she had begun, tending her business, keeping her house, guiding her husbands, and raising her daughters. She did nothing to insert herself into the politics of the Temple; she obeyed those Laws which were handed forth by the Thrice-Blessed, even when she, in her secret heart, deplored them.

When men were declared, not simply the lesser vessel, but a *flawed* vessel from which the Goddess averted her blessed gaze; when boys were expelled from the Temple schools; when more and younger husbands were placed within her household . . . she made no protest, though her heart whispered that these things were of the Temple and not of the Goddess.

When it came down as Law that the traders of Dayan might no longer trade with the pagan outworlders, save those who were female, or who came of families properly headed by a female; and might no longer trade with any ship, save those where captain and trader were properly female . . .

. . . *then*, she spoke. She testified before the Council of Seven, citing potential damage to trade, resulting in decreased profits, which would affect the Temple and the wider economy of Dayan.

For that testimony, she was given penance, for she had placed profit, and trade, and lowly mortal matters before the business of the Goddess. The penance was light, as she was both a Pillar and a Promise-Keeper, though for all of that a simple woman, more accustomed to dealing in the realm of the world. Her very simplicity had deceived her, and clouded her vision.

So ruled the Seven.

After serving her penance, Lomar Fasholt withdrew, a little, from public life; throwing all her energy in to what she knew best—trade. She was determined to preserve her household, provide for her husbands, and her daughters, though only one was young enough, still, to live beneath her mother's roof.

For it came about that she had not been deceived, and her vision had been as sharp as ever it had been, in matters of trade and profit.

The new restraints on trade had an instantaneous impact on the economy, as long-term contracts were canceled, and a dearth of properly configured families and ships was discovered. Those companies and ships that were located quickly understood their advantage, and for the first time in her life Lomar Fasholt saw money flowing away through her fingers like water.

Hers was not the only business that teetered; every trader on Dayan saw the same plummeting profits. Amis Delain, taking her lesson as a trader, and not as a child of the Temple, failed to terminate certain contracts with inappropriate sources, though she made no new contracts with such sources. Her losses were . . . less catastrophic than most—until the Thrice-Blessed realized that she had subscribed to a variant reading of the Law.

. . . Amis Delain, neither a Pillar nor a Promise-Keeper, but only a simple trader striving to maintain her house, and her husbands, and to creditably launch her daughters into adulthood . . .

Amis Delain was given seven strokes in the Temple foreyard, and fined half her worth.

Lomar protested this, as well, pointing out the verifiable, disastrous results of the new Law, pleading mercy for a young mother and rising trader.

The Seven commended her for her compassion; and fined her for disrespect of the Law.

It could have been worse; she might have been fined for blasphemy, or felt the lash along her own flesh.

As it was, it was bad enough, and Terbus forced to the strictest economies in order not to overrun their straitened finances. Lomar threw herself into her business, but without the outworld trade—without accepting that outworld folk had their own laws and customs, which were not of Temple or Goddess—there was no profit to be made.

Even worse, she could not reach the funds she, as a prudent trader would, banked off-world, at financial institutions that fell without the Law.

As resources on Dayan grew scarcer, she sold a piece of wooded land she had bought years ago, a solitary retreat where she might rest from her labors figuring vaguely in her thoughts. She would never have had such a thing constructed, or, were it built, use it—she loved her work too well to leave it. She had hopes of bolstering the house's finances by a half-year with that sale, but the real estate market was depressed, as well, and she sold at last to the Temple, for less than a quarter of its worth.

She struggled to maintain those things that were hers, did Lomar Fasholt, and her daughters did the same. There was talk of merging households, her daughters selling their houses, and returning to the home of their childhoods, thereby pooling their dwindling resources. But there was no one who would buy, save the Temple, which named its own price, and the Temple's price was never enough.

Still, there was peace, of a kind. The sort of stillness, so Lomar thought, that settled over the land immediately before a wind storm.

Then, the stillness broke.

Gilid Vyr, a trader slightly ahead of Fasholt in years and success . . . Gilid Vyr took her own life. Suicide being a sin, her property and possessions were taken by the Temple, which had no joy in the acquisition when it was learned that every stick of furniture had been sold, and the house itself pledged to the money-lenders at the Port, for a loan of staggering proportions.

The Temple cast off the loan, sowed the bereft and bewildered husbands among a half-a-dozen unrelated households. By the blessing of the Goddess, the adult daughters incurred no fines, having been found innocent of their mother's sin.

Swiftly on the heels of Vyr's suicide came the news that Temple's expenses outpaced its income. In light of this affront to the Goddess' glory, the Thrice-Blessed levied a tithe on all and everyone, consisting of three percent of each household's worth, as determined by the Temple.

It was this which saw Lomar Fasholt bent over her screen eating butter biscuits and drinking tea until her stomach churned.

She had paid the tithe, twice.

She could not pay a third time. *Could not*. The household had nothing more to give. Such funds as remained to Fasholt and Daughters were off-world, and beyond her reach.

That very morning, she had received a visit from a Thrice-Blessed, who had with scant courtesy informed her that she was in arrears. She had, with what patience she could muster, soothed somewhat by Terbus, who was serving tea and cakes, explained the house's situation. The Thrice-Blessed was . . . disinterested in such mundane matters as liquidity, a buyer's market, and a collapsed economy. She merely counseled the Temple's erring daughter that she ought take care, lest the Goddess be moved to extend Her Hand in anger.

The screen—the numbers . . .

Lomar pushed herself to her feet and stalked across the room, her eyes burning and her back muscles sore. Her gaze fell upon the Promise Chalice, in its place on the altar, green jade, and glowing with the power of her Promise to the Temple.

And what had she Promised as a Pillar? Why, to support the Temple in all its endeavors and to serve the Goddess as well as she might. She had then placed her hand on the jade chalice, and the Mother of Dayan Temple had placed her hand likewise, whereupon the chalice had taken fire from her Promise.

She stared at the chalice, at the beautiful thing that bound her to the Temple, and her secret heart wondered, not for the first time, why it was that her Promise had been first to the Temple, and only then to the Goddess Who was the Mother of All Creation and Who held the universe between Her two hands.

Behind her, the door opened, quietly. She turned, and met the eyes of her eldest husband, who stood empty-handed. It was not tea that had moved him, then, she thought, her heart warmed. Dear Teri; he knew her so well.

"Close the door," she murmured, and he did so, silently, before coming to her at the altar's edge.

"Is the household within walls?" she asked him.

"Sleak has gone with Daughter Aster to the stringed instrument showroom, this being the day that it's open to escorted males," he said, and then asked, lower, "Is it time?"

Lomar looked to the Chalice, glowing with the strength of her Promise, Teri's question echoing in her heart. *Was* it time?

The household had an Emergency Plan, of course—how not? She and Terbus had crafted the first iteration when it was only the two of them in the apartment over the office, inside the Port,

Lomar Fasholt, at trade in textile, spice, and exotics stenciled uncertainly on the front window.

As the house had grown, and the business, too, the upkeep of the Plan had fallen to Terbus. Every quarter, she would find a copy on her screen, revisions neatly highlighted; on her thumbprint, it was dispersed to all the household, even down to the youngest husband.

The question that remained now, and which yet troubled her heart—was this an emergency? The house was at risk, but so was all of Dayan. If, perhaps, she were to gather those other Pillars and Promise-Keepers to her, present a united front to the Temple, appeal the Law. Surely, faced with all, the Temple would—

BOOM!

She jumped, unable for an instant to place the sound, so seldom—and Teri was already across the office, moving at a run, portly as he had become, out the door, as the second *BOOM* sounded and she recognized it as the knocker striking the front door with considerable force.

Lomar started toward the door Terbus had left open in his wake—and now came a din of voices, motion in the hall, and suddenly the youngest husband, face pale, eyes wide, rushing back from the front of the house—

"Hearth-mother," he stuttered, "Mister Terbus says, *incoming*."

She stepped back into her office, then, recognizing the old code, dragging the boy with her, clearing the door barely ahead of her second-eldest husband, bearing what at first glance appeared to be an armful of bloodied rags. He paused, as if trying to decide where in her white-and-green office to dispose this burden, then strode forward to the very altar, which would take no lasting stain . . .

The bloody bundle moaned as it was lain down on the cool stone, and she knew it for her husband Sleak, musician and poet, face and chest slashed in a dozen places or more—

"Mother!" came a cry from the door, and here was Aster, supported by the fifth husband—her father, as it happened—her face smeared and her tunic torn, a rag pressed to the side of her head. Behind them came Terbus, with a med-kit, and the remainder of the husbands, bearing towels and absorbent pads.

"I fought them, Mother! I cut an initiate! The Temple—"

Lomar caught the girl's arms, pulling her away from the altar and the work going forth there. Aramis came with them, and she allowed it; he was a restful male, if not the brightest of the husbands, and Aster needed to be calmed.

"Tell me," she said, and the girl gulped and nodded.

"They were waiting for us when we came out of the showroom, and bore down upon us, shouting that Sleak had been rude, that he had pushed one of them, that if Fasholt didn't discipline her males, then it fell to them . . ."

She stopped on a shuddering gasp. Aramis rubbed her back and murmured wordless comfort until Aster had calmed sufficiently to continue.

"He hadn't—of course he hadn't! I protested, and stepped into their path— they, they tore the earring out of my—smashed my comm—and I struck her. Two were holding Sleak, and a third stripped off his shirt and—struck him—*cut* him! He tried to fold up, but he didn't fight! He struck no one! It was me; I cut them both, and grabbed him. We made the car, and I—I told it go home. I was afraid we'd be caught, if we tried to reach the hospital."

Lomar shivered, remembering the Thrice-Blessed "advice" of only that morning. The Goddess, was it? she thought, anger and fear mixing badly in her belly.

"You did what was required of you, in service of the house, and those who depend upon you," she told Aster, hugging her daughter to her, heedless of blood and grime.

She looked over the girl's head to Aramis.

"Tend her," she said, and he nodded, taking the shivering figure from her arms and gently steering her toward the couch. "Sit here, sweeting," he murmured. "I go for cleaning clothes, and the spray, for your poor ear . . ."

Dreading what she would see, Lomar stepped to the altar, where Terbus and Jeni worked over a pale, supine body.

Most of the blood had been cleaned away; and the worst of the cuts sprayed with sealant. A painkiller patch had been applied to the side of Sleak's neck, which accounted for his closed eyes and even breathing. Very nearly, Lomar regretted the lack of such an aid for herself.

Sleak was by far the prettiest of the husbands; he had the gift of music, and had been taught the tales. He was present at almost all of Fasholt's public entertainments, and his skill, no less than his looks, were the objects of wide admiration.

No longer.

Two dozen cuts at least, only on his face! His nose was broken by the look of it, and one cheekbone crushed. His chest and abdomen had also been slashed, but the work there was cursory, at best. The intent of the attackers had not been to kill, but to disfigure—and to terrify. But he was alive. Had he attempted to defend himself, matters might have gone far differently—but Sleak had always had a cool head, and it had served him well, even in terror.

"Will he be able to travel?" she murmured, for Teri's ear alone.

He looked in her eyes, nodded once.

"Communications?" she asked, and it was Jeni who answered that.

"Standard comms are non-functional. The ship-link is good."

She drew a breath, looked at them, bloody to their elbows; looked at the ragged boy on the altar.

"It's time," she said.

Teri nodded, and left the room, walking briskly, wiping blood away with a pad as he went.

Lomar turned to the face the room.

"Work clothes, everyone," she said, keeping her voice calm. "Those who have training should be armed. Follow the Emergency Plan. You have five minutes."

Praise to the Goddess, there was no outcry, no question. They had been trained well, her household. Her people. She would keep them safe.

She would.

They filed from the room, moving rapidly, with decision, but without panic.

Lomar was by design the last in the room, stopping at her desk to wipe the in-house databank, and to turn off the light over her desk.

That done, she followed the others, closing the door behind her.

In the room she left behind, the Promise Chalice glowed, richly green, over the disordered altar. Glowed . . . flickered . . .

And all at once shattered, jagged jade stuttering into gravel and raining down upon the blood-soaked towels.

TWO

Aequitas

Hel's Gate, Rannibic Station

Lomar called Terbus to her after supper; which would doubtless mean rumpled feelings to pat smooth next shift. She had adopted the strategy of sleeping alone in *Quitas'* master compartment for just that reason. It was, after all, a small ship, and her family numerous. The husbands were well-behaved; she allowed no pouting or preening in *her* household! But the truth was that, at home, there were daily tasks to fill their days, and she spent time with each, when business allowed, every moon.

On-ship, there was little in the way of chores that could be accomplished by untrained minds, though she was beholden to Pilot Manc for her creativity in dividing the necessary tasks of cooking, and wash up; the scrubbing of floors and the polishing of bright-work.

Terbus had of course been shipboard before, and he took up the role of supply clerk as if he had never stepped away from it.

And there it was—Terbus was eldest, and most experienced. He was a sensible man—a sensible *person*—with an understanding superior to many women she had known, though it had become blasphemy to speak such truths!

She desperately needed advice, and, yes, soothing, for her discoveries upon the day had unsettled her thoughts and her stomach equally.

So, she sent for Terbus, and when he arrived, sensibly attired in sweater and soft pants; ship-slippers on his feet, she felt some of the tension leach out of her shoulders, and she sighed.

He paused just inside the door, no longer the slim youth with the serious eyes her mother had picked out for her—a beautiful youth, of course, given her mother's predilections, but: "He's been trained to keep accounts," her mother had whispered, with a smile. "I do appreciate a man who is . . . multiply useful."

Multiply useful. Say rather indefatigably useful; she had never seen Teri at a standstill. Well, not until she brought home her last husband; that the Temple had chosen for her; and he was seen to be no older than Aster, herself still in the care of her tutors.

"May I bring you some wine, Hearth-mother?" Terbus asked, his voice mild, and his eyes downcast, the very picture of modest virtue.

Lomar laughed to see him so, and waved a hand.

"If you please, Mister Terbus—and bring a glass for yourself, also. In fact, bring the bottle! We will both want it, I think."

He bowed slightly, still coming the modest virgin, which pantomime continued to amuse her, as she moved across the small space, and brought the table out of the wall, and down, locking the legs into place.

By the time that was done, Terbus had returned, bearing the bottle, two glasses and an opener. He dealt expertly with all, pouring a little wine in the bottom of a glass and handing it to her for her opinion.

She laughed again, and shook her head. "We scarcely have so much wine that I'll send this bottle away, even if it proves to be vinegar!"

"If it is vinegar, we'll find a use for it in the kitchen," Terbus said imperturbably. "It is false economy to withhold what the Hearth-mother requires to keep us whole and safe."

"I believe that may be straight out of the Teachings," said Lomar.

"It may be," Terbus said; "I don't recall. Is the wine good?"

She tasted it, and sighed.

"In fact, it is very good," she said, holding out the glass. "Pour, Teri, and sit here beside me. I need your advice."

He did as she told him; sipped his wine when she sipped hers, and immediately put his glass on the table.

Lomar kept her glass in hand, and moved it slightly, watching the dark wine swirl.

"How is Sleak?" she asked, though that was not what she had called him here to talk about.

Terbus sighed.

"His outer hurts have healed," he said slowly. "But . . . his . . . mind is still unsettled. A few shifts ago, Jeni found him hiding beneath his bunk, shivering. He had awakened alone, and he feared an attack. It took Jeni more than an hour to coax him out. We keep watch now, and are certain that he has company at all times."

"Who is with him now?"

"Nathin."

She looked up sharply; Teri raised a hand to forestall her, which none of the others would dare.

"He's able, despite being so young; and Sleak seems to take a comfort from him that none of the rest of us can give."

"If he does not mend soon, tell me and I will find him a priestess," Lomar said.

Terbus shook his head.

"He is . . . particularly afraid that he will be brought to a priestess, and that he will be punished."

Lomar closed her eyes. It was reasonable, given what he had been through, that Sleak would fear such punishment. Yet it saddened her, that he had so little faith *in her*. She would go to him and show him that he was safe with her, as he had always been.

"I will see him, next shift," she told Terbus. "Please let me know when a visit will disrupt him least. I don't want him to live in fear."

"Yes," he said, and fell silent.

Lomar sipped her wine, and looked aside, thinking of Sleak, so handsome, and happy just to be making music . . .

"You were disturbed when you came back from the station," Teri said softly. "Aramis said you had found unhappy news at the Trade Bar."

She lifted her eyes to meet his.

"I hope he's not upset," she said, thinking back, but Aramis had seemed just as usual during their return to the ship. Of course, she *had* been disturbed, and might have failed to notice . . .

"Only because he had failed to shield you from distress," Teri said, extending a finger to touch his glass. "Aramis doesn't like to see anyone unhappy; you least of all."

Touched, she smiled.

"It was nothing he could shield me from, and no burden that any man is fit to carry. I had a plan, based on . . . old information, and a promise from . . . an associate." She shook her head, impatient with herself, raised her glass and drank half its contents in a single swallow, then put the glass away from her, leaned back against the bench, and looked directly into Teri's eyes.

"You recall the Master Traders yos'Galan," she said.

"Father and son," Teri said. His voice fell strangely on her ear with the phrase and she frowned slightly.

"Does that . . . trouble you, Teri?"

"Trouble me? No. It's so different from what's customary on Dayan that I find myself curious. I wonder what it would be like, to raise my own son, and teach him all that I know."

It was on the tip of her tongue to say that it would be very like raising daughters—but of course husbands did not raise daughters. That was for the Hearth-mother, tutors and elder sisters to do. Husbands *cared for* infant daughters, and minded toddler daughters; but husbands did not *teach* daughters.

And what, Lomar thought, would a husband teach his son? Well. Teri, of course, could keep accounts, and read, and organize—*Teri* had a score of useful and amusing skills. But . . . say, Aramis, who could neither read nor do sums; who had no skills at all, save the ability to be soothing. What could Aramis teach a son? Or young Nathin—who *could* read and figure, too, because Aster had taught him—but what could Nathin know, that was worth passing on?

"Are they well, the Masters yos'Galan?" Teri asked softly.

Lomar shook herself.

"The elder has entered the Garden of the Goddess, to receive his just rewards from Her hand," she said, only realizing as she said it that she assumed Er Thom yos'Galan would enter an afterlife that the Temple taught was exclusive to women.

"The son was well the last time I saw him, which was shortly after the Thrice-Blessed had decreed that we must trade only with ships and families and co-ops that were properly led by women. He *is* a master trader and he quickly grasped that such a Law could only bring disaster. At that point, he offered us his assistance in leaving Dayan. I had just recently spoken to the Thrice-Blessed myself, and still held some hope that, once they saw the havoc the Law produced, they would rescind it—so I refused his help. However . . ."

She raised her glass and sipped—and Teri did likewise.

"However, he left me with a final offer: That he would stake Fasholt and Daughters, if, later, we left Dayan, and would provide assistance in establishing ourselves and our brand in the wider galaxy." She sighed.

"I knew him to be honorable; and I knew that his clan was wealthy in those things that we would need, if we fled our home: money, and connections."

"You went to Rannibic Station to contact the young master and arrange a meeting." Teri said—not a question.

Lomar nodded.

"The pinbeam at the Trade Bar wasn't immediately available, so I took a booth, and called up the news archives." She raised her glass; lowered it and met Teri's eyes.

"This is how I learned that young Master Shan stood with his clan and the allies of his clan, including the Juntavas! Their were ships armed and threatening. One of their number—not the young master's ship—fired, on order of the delm of Shan's clan. Damage was done to the surface; people were killed . . ." She swallowed, raised her glass and drank deeply.

"As a result of this . . . attack, Clan Korval—that's the name of the young master's clan—was expelled from Liad, their homeworld, and their name struck from the Book in which all legitimate Liaden clans are numbered."

She put the glass on the table. Teri refilled it from the bottle.

"Clan Korval has relocated to Surebleak. *Dutiful Passage* has returned to the trade lanes; the routes of other Korval ships have been adjusted to accommodate the location of the new home port, and the edict which bans Korval ships from Liad. These things will have cost them money. Certainly, they will have lost allies, trade partners, connections . . ."

She shook her head, having run out of words, picked up her glass, thought better of it, and put it, carefully back down.

"And so I need your advice, Teri. Shall I assume that Shan yos'Galan is still the trader I knew, son of his father, shrewd and honorable?"

He considered her, brown eyes slightly narrowed.

"I am not a Hearth-mother," he said, slowly, "and though I may, once or twice, when I was an undisciplined and unruly youth, presumed to tell the wife into whose care the Goddess placed me what she ought do . . ."

Lomar laughed softly, remembering.

". . . I think that I understand the Hearth-mother's duty well enough to say that we do not want to associate ourselves with this master trader, even if he has retained all of his honor, and is canny enough to recoup his losses."

Lomar watched him raise his glass and sip.

"Why not?"

"Because," Teri said, "whether he and his family still have friends; they will have enemies, now—active enemies."

Fasholt needed friends, thought Lomar. In truth, they very nearly needed charity.

"Yes," she said. "Yes, you're correct. We don't need enemies—especially, we don't need borrowed enemies."

She looked at her glass, at the dark wine, glittering now and again with a reflected bit of light.

"What will you do?" Terbus asked.

She laughed, very softly, and raised the glass in a showy salute toward him.

"Pray," she said.

THREE

Aequitas
Hel's Gate
Rannibic Station

Prayer having yielded her nothing save the perverse conviction that she had been right in removing her family from the easy grasp of Dayan Temple, Lomar had recourse to her computer, her accounts, and the trade lists.

Lomar Fasholt was, after all, a trader, and a tradeship sitting idle at station was an expense she could not long afford. Rannibic Station did contain a market, but station goods were both exotic and expensive—no one went to a spacestation to buy wheat, after all. And the market-master was wise to keep his stock in the high end – fragile trinkets and handmades from little-visited worlds, aimed to capture the eyes of tourists—and much of the contents of their purses, as well.

Surprisingly, tourists came to Rannibic Station. Full-service hyatts, restaurants featuring "authentic" fare from a dozen worlds, and the so-called Fanuil Market existed to cater to those who booked guided drops to the planet's dead surface.

Indeed, tourism accounted for very nearly a fourth of Rannibic's revenues, more than anything else, except, of course, repairs.

Lomar Fasholt, however, was not a tourist; nor was she green; and, Goddess willing, her ship would not be found to require repairs while docked at one of the most comprehensive, and expensive, repair facilities in the sector. Therefore, her efforts were best focused on exchanging docking fees for profit.

That being so, she consulted with her pilot regarding routes and transit times, then hit the trade-lists, paying for the most recent data from the Trade Bar, though station management offered a good general list free to every ship that paid a docking fee.

List in hand, she consulted her accounts, projected expenses, with a percentage held back in case of emergency . . . consulted once more with Pilot Manc regarding routes, and likely ports, and again had recourse to the trade lists.

It was complex work, and soothing in its very familiarity. This was her calling, this her talent; and it was *this* that would preserve her family. She sank into the calculations, eventually emerging with orders for Pilot Manc, who immediately began negotiating a departure time with station.

Satisfied to see the results of her efforts being put into action, Lomar Fasholt stretched, smoothed her pink tunic, and went to visit her husband Sleak.

#

He was seated on his bunk when she entered, bent over the lute in his lap, his fingers moving over the strings so softly that she barely heard the notes.

Seated so, with his hair falling in a blue-black curtain past his shoulder, obscuring his face, he seemed for a moment to be precisely as he had been, when she had brought him into her household—Goddess, had it truly been twelve Standards ago?

He was a neatly made man, with a good leg, and long, brown feet that looked well in sandals. On those occasions when he was to entertain her guests, she dressed him to display those assets, and gave him rings to wear, so that his lithe fingers gleamed when he played. At those performances, he would wear his hair braided with silver ribbons, and she had seen many an eye linger on his clean profile and straight nose.

For her, though . . .

For her, he always played as he had played for her that first time: wearing a long, loose shirt, well-opened at the throat, and wide gauzy trousers, cuffed tight at the ankle; his long feet bare, and his hair unbound, making his face a mystery.

That first time . . . the music had held her rapt; his voice warmed her loins, and when he had at last raised his face to hers—ah, she had fallen in love with Sleak, as much for his beauty as for his art. He had been a luxury; Terbus, Jeni, and Vroyd were by no means over-burdened, but once she had seen him; once she had partaken of his art—well, she had to have him.

Once she had him, of course, she made use of him, to the profit of the house, for even twelve Standards ago, a man trained in the classic songs and the old stories had been . . . a novelty among the younger women. Among those of Lomar's age and older, who could remember a time when men kept 'count books and could read as well as any daughter, he had been a taste of sweet nostalgia.

Now?

Now, Sleak was a rarity. Possibly he—and Terbus, and Jeni, who was trained as a medic—were blasphemies.

And what, she thought suddenly, would Sleak pass on to *his* son? His songs? The old stories that he was forbidden, now, to know? The many ways that one might coax a lute to speak?

The music whispered into silence. For a long moment, Sleak kept his pose, lute cuddled on his lap, head bent, as if considering whether or not he would play some other song.

Then, of a sudden, he raised his head, flinging his hair back over his shoulder with a gesture that seemed almost . . . defiant.

His face . . . the gashes were healed, but there were scars; a pale webwork overlaying his warm brown features like a mask. She had known that there had been scaring; Jeni had told her that newly healed wounds were yet vulnerable. Later . . . later, they would erase the scars, but for now, they must be careful not to endanger Sleak's health.

But it wasn't the scars that made him seem so altered.

It was his eyes.

Black, and hard as glass; his gaze cold.

Angry.

Well, and it would scarcely be the first time Sleak had been angry; his moods were as volatile as his music. And surely, Lomar thought, coolly meeting that angry gaze—surely anger was superior to fear.

"Well, my Sleak?" she said, her voice as cool as her gaze.

"No, not well!" he snapped, and thrust his face forward. "Unless you prefer this?"

"I do not, and I am not the cause of it."

He gasped as if she had struck him, and snapped to his feet, turning to place the lute gently on the bunk, and swinging back toward her with so much energy that Lomar flinched, and felt a spark of her own temper.

"Are you not the cause of it?" Sleak demanded, his voice low and rough. "Who angered the Temple? Who put her House in peril? Who broke troth, that she pledged before the Goddess Herself?"

"I did not break troth!" she snapped. "Mine was not the hand that struck you!"

"You swore. You swore to keep me safe; and never let harm befall me." He took a hard breath, and turned, showing her his back.

"You failed."

Those two words would have cut less deeply, had they been forged of steel.

"You will turn and face me," she said, letting anger be heard while she kept the hurt pressed tight against her heart.

For a moment, she thought his anger would lead him into error, and she did not—she very much did not wish to discipline him, at this hour, and in this condition. So, she did not repeat the order, merely waited.

Sleak turned, but it was no bashful smile he showed her, only those same icy eyes caught in the pale net of his scars.

"You broke troth," he said again. "What will you do, to repair it?"

Well, there was a question from the old songs. And yet, Lomar thought, her own anger cooling a little, he was, in a sense, correct. Not that she had broken troth —that was anger and fear speaking, and he would know better, when he was less distraught. But, she *had* displeased the Temple. More, she had known it.

That she had not understood that the Thrice-Blessed would offer violence to a defenseless member of her House, rather than deal with one better able to protect herself—that did not excuse her. For the Hearth-mother kept the hearth peaceful, and warm, and insured the good health of those she had taken in care.

In that sense, Sleak was correct: She had failed in the most basic, and the most important of her duties.

He was watching her still, her disfigured husband; his cold anger showing no sign of thaw. Soft words would not mend this;

nor, as Terbus had said, and which she now saw was wisdom, would a promise to find him a Priestess, for healing.

Sleak had put his pain and his anger before her—which the Temple taught was his part. It was for her, to mend this for him . . .

And one line from an old song surely deserved another.

"What then would you have your Wife do, best beloved?"

His mouth tightened, as if her words had tasted bitter; but he did not avert his gaze when he said, "I would be trained to use weapons—gun, knife, and fists—so that I may protect *myself* against any who would harm me."

That *was* blasphemy. Even when Terbus had learned to shoot, so many years ago—even then, it was taught that it was a far better thing for the weaker vessel to depend upon the protection of Wife and Daughters, for had not the Goddess given men into the keeping of women?

And what was blasphemy? Lomar thought, the thought itself carrying a sense of danger, as if she held a wine glass by a cracked stem. At any moment, the stem might complete its own destruction, gashing her fingers, and splattering her with wine.

Lomar took a deep breath. She did not look away from her husband Sleak, and she kept her voice gentle.

"I understand your desire, but I ask you, my Sleak, to think on this question: What would have befallen you—you and all of our House—had you struck, wounded, or—Goddess forfend—killed one of the women who attacked you?"

His cold eyes widened; his lips parted.

Lomar nodded.

"I ask you to meditate upon that, as I will meditate on those things you have said to me. In two ship-days, at this hour, you will come to me in my cabin, and we will speak again."

She held out her hand for his kiss.

Sleak closed his eyes, and turned his head aside.

"I will come to your cabin in two ship-days, at this hour," he said, his voice flat, then edged, throwing the last two words as if they were knives, "*Hearth-mother*."

Lomar stared at the side of his face. When he did not move, or open his eyes, she turned and put her hand against the door.

"Husband," she said; "I bid you good-day."

* * *

He was playing the lute again when the boy arrived to bear him company. He was late, which was often the case with the boy, but Sleak did not draw the lapse to his attention. Truth said, he had been glad enough of the time alone, after his Wife, who was, so he was taught by the oldest song he knew, the Goddess enfleshed and the keeper of his soul, had left him alone with her terrible question.

No sooner had the door closed behind her than his strength had failed, and he had fallen to his knees, weeping in terror and remorse. Terror, because terror was his constant companion since he had risen from the autodoc, and remembered what had befallen him.

And remorse?

Remorse because Lomar was a good woman; a good Wife, so far as he might judge, who knew all the psalms exalting the Wifely virtues. A good woman who had struck him only once, when he was young and testing his power over her, so much his elder and so clearly besotted. Struck him she had then, once, and strongly, and banished him from her bed and from the community table for an entire First Moon. He'd been angry then, too, and thought he wouldn't care.

But he *had* cared, and when he went to her after his punishment was done, he knew himself happier to be in her light than cast out of it.

He was older now, and knew Wife Lomar well: strong, and stubborn, and fiercely intelligent; light-humored; even-handed, even when her temper was roused. He knew the pride she took in her daughters, and the joy imparted by her work. She was not a woman to break a promise, much less a holy oath given to the Goddess, before the whole of the Temple.

Yet, she *had not* kept him safe, and his heart argued that his anger was just. It had seemed so clear, when he had lain on his bunk, thinking about what had happened, and how to ensure that it never happened again. If Wife Lomar would or could not protect him, and if he refused ever again to be abused by those who wished her ill, then he must learn to protect himself.

And yet, if he had snatched an assailant's knife, used it against her? Hurt her? *Killed* her?

What would have befallen you and all our House? That was the question she left him with, knowing that he knew the answer. There were songs, and poems, that told of such transgressions; he had learned them, though he never sang them. And those songs also told of the Temple's Justice.

Had he struck or scored one of his attackers, his life would have been forfeit, and all the lives of his brother husbands, for if one was a blasphemy, then all were tainted. Lomar herself would have been whipped before the Temple entire, before she, too, was executed. Aster, yet a Maiden, would likely have been spared, and taken into the Temple as a novice. The other daughters, married all . . . if the Thrice-Blessed had determined the taint had spread . . .

Dozens might have been returned to the Goddess, if Sleak had dared to raise his hand to strike one blow in his own defense.

He moaned, then, in horror, and climbed into the bunk, curling his body around the lute, and pulling the blankets over his head. Eventually, his tears ran out, and, exhausted, he slept, waking some little while later to find it near time for the boy's visit.

He washed his face, averting his gaze from the mirror, and combed his hair by touch, before ordering the blankets and taking a seat on the bunk, the lute on his lap. By the time the boy did arrive, he was playing, softly, a song of his own composing.

"Day-chef sends lunch, since you didn't come to table," Nathin said, offering a hot-box and a thermos.

Sleak considered them warily.

"Day-chef was Ronlath?" he asked, naming the seventh husband, notorious for his lack of ability in the kitchen.

Nathin shook his head.

"Vroyd."

"Well, Vroyd is an entirely different matter," Sleak said, forcing lightness into his voice. "Set them on the desk, child; I'll sup in a little while."

"It really is good," Nathin said, doing as he was told. "You'll want to eat it, and not only because Jeni will be after you if you don't."

"I will eat it," Sleak promised, his fingers moving over the strings.

Nathin sat on the opposite end of the bunk, his back against the wall and one knee crooked onto the bed.

"Mister Terbus said that the Hearth-mother had visited you, and that was likely why you had missed the meal."

Sleak snorted lightly, though Teri's assumption hadn't been wrong, after all.

"*Did* the Hearth-mother visit?" Nathin pursued. "We don't see much of her, since coming a-ship. Aster says she's busy looking out for us, and laying in a route to make money, and find us a new home."

Daughter Aster and Nathin were close in age, the youngest in the household; and shared a bond like that between brother husbands. It worried Terbus, who, as Eldest Husband was in charge or worrying. It ought, in Sleak's opinion, also worry Lomar, but she gave no sign that she saw anything . . . dangerous.

Sleak, who was fond of the boy, sang him songs about a husband's duties to the Wife, but it was difficult to know how much took root in the young head, most especially since the Wife had not taken the boy to her bed.

"It must be a difficult and busy time for her," he said, his fingers moving of their own will over the strings.

"Yet she came to visit you!" Nathin said, never one to be shaken from a topic that had gained his interest. "Was it well?"

Was it well? That was what the older husbands asked each other after a visit from the Hearth-mother. The child had no idea what he was asking, and Sleak should merely have smiled, and said that yes, it was well.

Instead, he raised his head and meant the bright blue eyes.

"No, it was not well. I was angry."

Nathin blinked.

"Angry? Angry about—oh! But, you've been hurt and healing up! She didn't want to visit until you were well; Jeni told Aramis he had suggested that the Hearth-mother give you time to rest. And I told you, none of us sees much of her of late!"

The child thought he had been angry because Lomar had not visited him before this. He might have taken that path, too, and let the boy reside a while longer in innocence, but Sleak had never lied to Nathin, and, today of all days, he did not wish to begin.

"I wasn't angry that she hadn't visited," he told the boy, and glanced down at the strings, as though his fingers didn't know their business. "I was angry because she had . . . allowed me to be hurt. I demanded—*demanded*, you see, not asked—that I be taught weapons-lore, and hand-to-hand fighting."

"But that's women's work!"

And so it was, now. And so Sleak should only have nodded, and sung a riddle song for the boy's amusement, and perhaps another, before he opened the hot-box and ate the meal Vroyd had kindly sent to him.

But, the songs existed; songs that he knew, some terrible, most not—songs that he practiced, and never sang for any but himself. And it came to him that, should he die, those songs would die, too; falling out of memory like a sudden rainstorm, all forgotten in a moment.

He could not bear it, if the songs—if the histories—were forgotten; he shuddered with sudden fear for them.

"Sleak?" The child leaned forward and touched his hand, and immediately he felt calmer. That decided him, for the boy was a treasure, with his calming touch, which would never be properly brought to fruition, since the Temple taught that only females had the gift of healing. Sleak knew better; the songs spoke of others like Nathin. The boy should be told that, at least.

At least.

"Back in olden times," he said, shifting the lute so that he could work the pegs. "In olden times, men bore weapons, and were trained in their best use. In olden times, men were able to do many things—read, and figure; heal and foretell. They were not all tied to a house, nor bound to a Hearth-mother; they ranged free, and managed themselves."

Nathin's eyes were the size of soup tureens.

"Is that—how do you know that?"

"The songs," Sleak told him. "It's in the songs."

"But, the songs—they're not true! They're just . . ."

"History. The songs are true. Part of my . . . work was to research the songs; to find the histories that grew them. I did that until the archives were closed to us, and the Temple decreed that only women might learn the oldest songs, or search for lost lyrics in the old books.

"There are songs that relate a whole history of an actual event. You've heard me sing the Virtues, haven't you?"

Nathin nodded.

"Those are teaching songs. Some songs refer to an event through imagery and allegory, but once those are pulled aside, and the actual event uncovered in history, it's found to tell a straight tale.

"I know a song that tells the true history of Lady Moonhawk, a priestess of the Temple, and how she came to be the apprentice of a traveling show magician; a man named Lute." He paused a moment to give attention to his tuning, then looked up and smiled into Nathin's eyes.

"Would you like to hear it?"

Nathin took a deep breath, nodded jerkily, and then said, "Yes. Yes, I would like to hear it, please, Sleak."

"Then you shall, in only a moment. It's a very old song, and requires a tuning different from what I usually . . ."

He paused, the fear stirring again in his belly, and perhaps the glance he sent then into the boy's eyes was fiercer than he intended, for the lad flinched, then straightened.

"Peace," Sleak murmured. "It has only just come to me that this song is known . . . to very few; and is never sung. I would ask you to listen hard, and remember the words, so if . . . if something happens to me, the song will have a home."

Nathin gave a solemn nod. "I will remember," he said. "I have a very good memory."

Goddess bless the boy, he did, too.

Sleak smiled, and tested his tuning, his fingers moving deliberately into the opening phrase.

"Here, then, is the *Ballad of Lute and Moonhawk*."

From Every Storm A Rainbow

Sinit Caylon, delm-elect of Clan Mizel, gazed across the table at Peers dea'Gauss.

Peers gazed back, face non-committal. Neither looked at the third member of their party, Sinit's mother, Birin Caylon, who was Mizel-in-Truth . . .

. . . for another four years. Then, by the terms of the agreement signed with Clan Korval, Sinit would take up Mizel's Ring, clan administration, management of its assets, fiscal, physical, and corporeal. Mizel had signed because her hand had been forced two Standards ago, but she was not reconciled.

The same agreement placed Peers dea'Gauss into Mizel as a consultant, taking up what would, in a less emperilled clan, be the duties of the nadelm. In the proper order of things, Sinit would be nadelm–but, no. Sinit Caylon would *never* have been nadelm, if Mizel had been in proper order. And, she realized, Peers was waiting for her answer.

"I reviewed the precis you gave me," she said, placing her hand on that document where it rested on the table before her. "In addition, I went back through the accounts to the beginning of my great-grandmother's term of service—"

Her mother tapped her fingers on the table, impatient, meaning, perhaps to distract. However, Sinit had been taking lessons in maintaining one's countenance under provocation from a master, and did not allow herself so much as a pause.

"—in order to identify the moment of error."

Peers inclined her head.

"And did you find the moment, my lady?"

Sinit patted the precis gently, as if it were one of Lady yo'Lanna's large, indolent dogs.

"I see that my great-grandmother and my grandmother kept diversified portfolios and were aggressive in moving funds from under-performing shares. They both kept reserves in conservative funds, but even those monies might be moved to another location, if the terms were sufficiently lucrative, and the fund itself of a high order."

Sinit took a breath and did not look at the present delm, who had stopped tapping the table, which was in someway *more* distracting.

"I found the error was not a single event, but an accretion; a pattern of behavior that began to have adverse effects on the clan's financial security approximately twelve years into the stewardship of the current delm."

She took a deep breath, embracing inner calm.

"The previous delm's arrangements had not been altered—there was no need; the markets were stable. Mizel's fortunes trended slightly downward, not enough to be thought worrisome. They may have easily recovered, had the markets boomed.

"There was a collapse in the fourteenth year of the present delm's service. The old arrangements were no longer viable. A radical change of financial strategy was necessary." Sinit took another breath, and spoke directly to Peers, as if there was no third at their table.

"Change was not made, and Mizel's fortunes declined, rapidly."

There, it was said. Sinit reached for her teacup. She sipped, awaiting an outburst of chill rage from her parent, and—still—her delm.

None came.

Peers inclined her head.

"Indeed, you have identified the moment when required action was not taken. From that point, recovery became more difficult every year. Is it your opinion, my lady, that recovery is beyond us?"

Sinit knew Peers well enough by now to know that this was a test.

She put her teacup aside.

"Not beyond us," she said slowly, "though I do not make the error of believing recovery will be quick or easy. We will need to be canny and flexible. This is where I depend upon you, Ms. dea'Gauss."

That was nothing more than the truth. If Sinit was going to rebuild Mizel's foundation and standing—as she must!—she was going to need someone very like Peers dea'Gauss as an ally. How Mizel would afford her fees once the six year term was up, Sinit hadn't the least notion. She hoped something would occur to her—well. It would *have to*, wouldn't it?

"Your ladyship is kind," Peers murmured. "Perhaps you see a target upon which I may train my canniness?"

Sinit reached for the ledger where all of Mizel's accounts were listed out. Her mother sighed sharply. Sinit did not glance aside.

"I believe," she said to Peers, "that we must begin by divesting ourselves of certain properties, not only to increase our treasury, but to lighten the burden of our obligations."

She opened the ledger to the place she had marked, and turned the book toward Peers.

"How dare you!" Mizel erupted. "Golindor Manufacturing has been a cornerstone of the clan's wealth since before your great-grandmother took up the Ring! Will you sell our history?"

"No, ma'am," Sinit said, turning to meet the delm's eyes. She had gotten quite good at meeting anger with calm. That had perhaps been Lady yo'Lanna's most useful lesson thus far.

"Golindor will always be a part of Mizel's history. Indeed, it must be held up as a lesson to future delms and nadelms, for the delm's hand was as deft as her eye was sure. Mizel's long-term stability, which serves us even now, may surely be lain to that acquisition."

She looked down at the sad ledger, the profits line near to plunging off the bottom of the page, while the expense line sought the upper margins.

"In present, ma'am, as you can see, expenses far outstrip profits. Mizel cannot make needed upgrades. Now is the time to sell, while there is still some value left."

"I do not agree to this," Mizel said.

Peers looked to her.

"Of course, it is never pleasant to liquidate assets, but in the case, it is the best for the property and for the clan. I will, if you wish, prepare a report to the oversight committee, presenting Lady Sinit's solution, and your disagreement. Your ladyship surely knows that the committee will debate, but allow the liquidation. Meanwhile, the property will become less attractive."

Mizel glared at Peers, her eyes cold.

"Certainly, we should not wish to bring ourselves to the notice of *the committee*. You make your point eloquently, as usual, *Qe'andra* dea'Gauss."

She stood, waving a hand that seemed too frail for the burden of Mizel's Ring.

"Please, continue with your pleasant plans, *delm-in-waiting*. You have no need of me for this."

She left them, closing the study door gently behind her.

Sinit sat, hands folded tightly in her lap while she examined her actions and intent. After a moment, she was able to admit to herself that she had not acted in malice, nor to cause distress, but for the best good of the clan, insofar as she could judge. Lady yo'Lanna's brother, Delm Guayar, had been adamant regarding the on-going necessity of such evaluations. "For we are none of us infallible, and it is not beyond us to be petty. It is therefore the first duty of we who hold the good of our clans cupped in our palms to be certain of our motives."

"My lady?" Peers murmured. "May I ask after your thoughts?"

Sinit raised her head.

"I was thinking that my mother looks . . . ill," she said, which was not . . . wholly . . . untrue. "This—the transition—is not easy for her."

"No, my lady," Peers said. She paused. "Shall we continue?"

"Yes," Sinit looked back to the journal page.

"Golindor must be liquidated," she said. "I wish to sell quickly, and as advantageously as possible. When it is done, I wish you will review the process with me."

Peers raised her eyebrows. Sinit felt her face heat.

"What I mean to say is that I must look forward to the day when you will not be available to me. I would learn how to make such decisions."

"Ah." The *qe'andra* inclined her head. "I will be pleased to teach the method, my lady, though I feel I must point out that my canniness is at your service for a few years, yet."

"Yes," Sinit agreed, looking down at the ledger again. "But you and I both know that when I take the Ring, the agreement ends, and Mizel will be in no position to afford you."

That was rather plainly said, but Peers, improbably, smiled.

"No, my lady, you must allow me to work. It is my goal that Mizel will be very well able to afford me, when the Ring passes."

Sinit frowned, recalling her recent review of Mizel's financials.

"I would not have thought that you were an optimist," she said.

"I am a realist, my lady. To the business at hand, you have made a bold and necessary first move to bring Mizel back from the edge. Have you given thought to your follow?"

Sinit bit her lip. But, really, if she could not bring this to Peers, who was required by contract hold Mizel's prosperity as her first priority, then who?

"I wonder if you will advise me?"

"Of course, my lady."

Sinit smiled.

"Then I will tell you that I have a goal. I had been used to thinking of it as part and parcel of restoring Mizel's finances, but lately I have been thinking of assets, and I wonder if we might not achieve this thing separately, and sooner, for it will be years before Mizel is restored."

Peers frowned slightly.

"A few years, my lady. Recall that the agreement has Korval remitting the life-price of a scholar-expert to Mizel when the Ring passes. That is not an inconsiderable sum."

"I do recall that," Sinit said. "But this other thing—I do not wish to wait four more years to bring Mizel's children home!"

Peers blinked.

"Well, they're scarcely children any more," Sinit rushed on. "Tiatha—my sister Aelliana's heir—is very nearly as old as I am, and Ver Non—Voni's heir—not so many relumma behind. Jes and

Zilli are younger, but long out of the nursery. The delm had good reason to foster them to Lydberg, but—"

She paused, realizing that she was out of countenance.

"Your pardon. This matter has weighed on me since the delm spoke of marrying Lydberg as the lesser partner. In short, I want our children brought home. They are Mizel's treasures, so much more so than—" She slapped her hand on Golindor's ledger page.

There was a brief silence. Peers inclined her head.

"I understand, my lady. However, the fosterings were done by Mizel's will. They must be dissolved by Mizel's will."

And she was not—yet—Mizel. Sinit sighed.

"I think—I think that my mother might be better served, were there people in the house—kin. To live here alone—" *with the ghost of her favorite child her only companion*— "I think it cannot be—good for her."

She paused. Peers waited.

"I will speak with her," Sinit said, "when she is in a better frame of mind. I think she might agree to bring them home, if only I can show her the way."

"I understand," Peers said. "I will work with your goal in mind."

#

Despite having been late at Etgora's evening gather, Sinit was up early with her schoolwork. She had completed the basic coursework, and stood within a relumma of finishing the advanced course. Then she would put her name before the Accountant's Guild as an apprentice. Her goal was to have a secure place in one of the established firms before Mizel's Ring was on her hand. The

House would need her income, and the expertise she gained could only assist in accomplishing her duties as delm.

There came a rap at the door.

Sinit rose, crossed the room, and opened to Ms. pel'Ena the butler.

"This came express, Lady Sinit," said that august person, offering an envelope.

Sinit glanced at it, recognizing Mizel's seal—the Thundercloud and Rainbow—and felt her stomach clench. There were only four, now, who would use that seal— herself, her eldest sister Voni, her mother, and her delm.

Voni was not given to writing, being so very busy with her duties as a hostess at the Middlemarch Mountain Ski Resort.

It was equally unlikely that her mother would write—but, no, Sinit reminded herself. Her mother had been very sensible during their last talk. Indeed, she had been eager to see Mizel's children brought back to their proper place, going so far as to promise to consult the delm.

This note could be the result of that consultation. It might, Sinit told herself, be good news.

She took the envelope with a small bow.

"Thank you, Ms. pel'Ena."

"Always of service," the butler replied. "Shall I send a tray up? There's the buffet this morning."

Justus was a busy clan, and breakfast was often a buffet, to accommodate the many diverging schedules.

"Please," Sinit said, the letter weighing in her hand. "That would be pleasant."

Ms. pel'Ena bowed and went away. Sinit returned to her desk, and broke the envelope's seal.

It was . . . not . . . good news.

She might have thought it a joke, save that neither her mother nor her delm indulged in humor.

The agreement stated specifically that Sinit Caylon would *not* receive lessons in administration from Clan Korval. However, the agreement did not forbid her from speaking to her sister, who was, coincidentally, the delmae of Korval.

The comm signaled twice, bringing Sinit to an awareness of the hour. She moved to cut the connection, but too late.

"Good morning, Sinit," came the cool, firm voice. "Did you enjoy a good sleep?"

"Aelliana," she said, tears starting to her eyes. "Mizel has gone to Low Port."

#

"For what purpose?" Lady yo'Lanna asked. She was in the New Garden, trowel in hand, placing seedlings in a fresh-turned bed.

Sinit dropped to her knees, so as not to be greater than her host, and met the lady's eyes.

"She says to find the nadelm, and bring him back to fulfill his proper place."

"Mizel's nadelm is dead," Lady yo'Lanna stated.

"By the Delm's Word, yes, ma'am. But she never reconciled—"

"I mean to say," Lady yo'Lanna interrupted, "that Ran Eld Caylon is *dead* in the most physical sense possible. Low Port is dangerous even to those who reside there. It is inimical to strangers."

"I spoke to Aelliana. She assures me of these same things," Sinit admitted, leaving aside the other things Aelliana had said. "She has an . . . associate, whom she will ask to locate Mizel, and return her to her proper location."

Lady yo'Lanna bent her head, perhaps recruiting herself, for Mizel's actions must surely horrify so stringently proper a lady.

"And your own plans?" her ladyship asked.

"I am for Raingleam Street, ma'am, with all speed. The House—"

"Indeed," Lady yo'Lanna said, suddenly brisk. "The House."

She rose, stripping off her gloves. Sinit came also to her feet, extending a hand to the gardening basket.

"No, leave it, child," her ladyship said. "Let us see you on your way."

#

The house was empty when she arrived, early in the afternoon. Well, of course it was. The servants had long ago been turned off, for lack of funds to pay them. Aelliana was lifemated, Voni was at her employment, Ran Eld was dead, and Mother—

Sinit swallowed as she went through the lower floor, opening doors and turning on lights. At the delm's office, she paused with her hand on the door.

Eyes closed, she reviewed her motives. Satisfied that this was a necessary action, she turned the knob—and entered a scene of chaos.

The delm's desk, usually so tidy, was awash in loose sheets and notebooks, as if the contents of all the drawers had been emptied onto it. There were books on the floor—the bound set of the *Liaden Code of Proper Conduct*, Sinit saw, detouring carefully around them on her way to the desk.

She considered the mess, keeping her hands behind her back. The notebooks were sharesbooks, the loose sheets, ledger pages. Sinit bit her lip. Had *she* precipitated this, with her talk of bringing the children home?

She leaned closer, seeing a gleam of color among the ledger pages, in the style of a clan seal.

Taking hold of the sheet with careful fingertips, she gently pulled it free.

It was Lydberg's seal. The note was abrupt; apparently in response to a letter from Mizel.

It is gratifying that Mizel has at last recalled its inconvenient baggage. Lydberg is willing to return it, upon receipt of upkeep costs on the order of three cantra. Be this amount received by Trianna Eighthday of the current relumma, the baggage shall be released to Mizel.

If Mizel remains in default on Zeldra Eighthday, the contracts will be sold at Lydberg's discretion, all wages therefrom coming to Lydberg until such time as the debt has been paid in full.

This by the hand of Lydberg Herself

Three cantra! Sinit felt her breath hitch in panic.

But, no. Panic was not an option, not now. She must solve this. When the debt was retired, and the children safe in Mizel's house, *then* she would panic.

Think, she told herself. Lydberg's letter was meant to intimidate, to demonstrate Mizel's weakness and lack of resource while explicitly placing Mizel's children in peril.

But Mizel *had* resources.

Sinit placed the letter on top of the chaos that was the delm's desk, and sought the comm in the library. The comm was answered immediately.

"Ms. dea'Gauss," Sinit said, stringently calm. "I need you to come to Raingleam Street at your earliest opportunity. It is a matter of some urgency."

#

She opened the door to the delm's office and stepped back to allow Peers to enter.

The *qe'andra* walked carefully, avoiding, as Sinit had, the books on the floor, and standing over the desk with her hands behind her back.

She turned around.

"Did you touch anything, my lady?"

"The letter, there on top, from Lydberg. It had been under that muddle of ledger pages on the right. I saw the clan seal and thought—" Embarrassingly, her voice hitched again. "I thought it might provide a clue as to why the delm left us."

"Indeed," Peers said dryly. "Forgive me, my lady, but I wonder if you know where Mizel has gone."

Sinit closed her eyes.

"The delm has gone to Low Port," she said, pleased that her voice was perfectly even and in-mode. "Her reason was to find Mizel's once-was nadelm and fetch him home."

She took a breath, and opened her eyes. Peers was watching her calmly, waiting.

"Lady yo'Lanna states as fact that Ran Eld Caylon is dead to all and everything. My sister—has asked grace of an associate, who may, perhaps, be able to locate the delm and . . . *extract her*—" that had been Aelliana's exact phrase—"before she finds harm."

Sinit spread her hands. "The delm did write to me of her intent. The letter found me this morning. It is why I'm here."

"Of course," Peers murmured. "How may I serve you, my lady?"

Sinit sighed. "Advise me—Lydberg threatens Mizel's children. Surely, they must be answered, quickly and firmly."

"Surely, they must," Peers said, plucking the letter from atop the pile. "Let us take this to our usual table. First, I will use the comm. The oversight committee must be told."

Sinit sighed as they exited the room.

"Yes, of course. I should have told them, but I thought it best to first secure the House."

"You have the instincts of a delm, and you have done everything that is proper," Peers said, firmly. "You secured the House, and you called your *qe'andra*. Your *qe'andra* will now call the committee, which task is her explicit duty."

Sinit reached around Peers to close the door.

"Are they likely to send someone?"

"They may, though I cannot say how quickly. In fact, I will make another call. This is an unusual situation, and I would consult with an elder of my firm. If they deem it necessary to send someone, *that* person will arrive quickly."

Excellent, thought Sinit, and did *not* think of how Mizel would afford the expense.

"While you make your calls, I will make tea," she said. "Find me at our usual table, when you are able."

#

"Definitely, a threat has been lain here."

The elder from the firm, Etha dea'Gauss, seemed inclined to take a very dark view of this. She had arrived with astonishing quickness, and sat now with a cup of tea by her hand, notetaker to the fore.

"My first thought had been to stall," Peers murmured. "My second was that such tactics might create greater peril. Lydberg's timeline gives us room to work."

"Your second thought is worthy, young Peers. Immediately, we should send a acknowledgment of receipt, which will also inform Lydberg that Mizel is taking counsel from our firm. More than that is not necessary. As you say, the given deadline, while not generous, allots us some time to work."

She sipped her tea. "It falls to you as Mizel's *qe'andra* of record to acknowledge Lydberg. Do so. Lady Sinit and I will begin discovery."

"Yes." Peers rose, bowed, and left them.

Etha dea'Gauss finished her tea, and set the cup aside.

"Do you have a copy of the contract with Lydberg, my lady?"

Sinit sighed.

"I regret. There is no contract."

Ms. dea'Gauss inclined her head.

"One has heard that there has been a certain . . . reticence on the part of the current delm with regard to sharing documentation. Perhaps Mizel's former *qe'andra* will have a copy among their dead files. If your ladyship does not recall the name, I will query the Guild. Indeed, I should have done so before I came to you."

Sinit put her palms flat on the table, and met Ms. dea'Gauss's eyes.

"My mentor has long since despaired of my tendency for plain speaking ma'am. I assure you that I do not mean to be . . .

unconvenable. I merely wish to be certain that information is conveyed with clarity."

Etha dea'Gauss eyed her.

"Certainly, my lady. Clarity of information must be our goal in this and all of our of transactions."

"Plainly, then—if Mizel retained a *qe'andra* prior to Peers—I mean to say, Ms. dea'Gauss—it was before my birth. As the arrangement we now confront was made *after* my birth, there is no need to disturb the cellars of the Accountants Guild."

She paused, the elder said nothing. Sinit inclined her head.

"There is no contract with Lydberg, ma'am. However, I *can* tell you how the arrangement was made."

"Please proceed, my lady."

Sinit reached for her cup, and sipped tea to ease her dry throat.

"When my mother was young, she was sent to live for a year with our cousins Clan Lydberg, while a child of Lydberg came to Mizel. It was a done thing, when my grandmother was a girl, and she felt that her heir should also receive the benefit of being fostered into another House. While she was with Lydberg, Mother and Voni pel'Dina became fast friends. The friendship outlasted the fostering. Mother named the first of her children who remained in-House after her friend, who was said to have done the same."

Sinit paused for another sip of tea.

"When Mizel realized that the House was unable to care for the nursery, Mother turned to her friend for advice. Between them, they crafted a solution—that Lydberg would foster Mizel's next generation. This arrangement was intended to be in force for only a year, perhaps two, until the clan came about."

She paused; Etha dea'Gauss inclined her head.

"Mizel never recovered sufficiently to bring the children back into the House, and mother's friend continued to keep them safe, in hers."

Sinit turned her palms up.

"Voni pel'Dina is Lydberg's sister, she had his ear and his support. It seems apparent that Mizel offended by writing, yet—"

"Lydberg's Ring passed twelve days ago," Etha dea'Gauss said gently. "Voni pel'Dina clearly does not have the support of the new delm."

Sinit blinked.

"I—saw the announcement in the *Gazette*," she said. "I should have realized that there would be—change."

"No, how could you?" said the elder, briskly. "Unless you are privy to Lydberg's internal politics?"

Sinit laughed.

Ms. dea'Gauss smiled. "Exactly. Now, my lady, attend me. This situation did not grow from the seeds of your errors."

"That is true," Sinit said, "it only falls to me to—to—*fix this*!" she burst out, which was surely unworthy from one who would be delm.

"It falls to *us* to fix it—yourself, supported by your *qe'andra*. We *will* arrive at an equitable solution. May I ask what your plans are, while Mizel is absent?"

"I will hold the House until the delm returns," Sinit said, wondering what other plans she might have.

Etha dea'Gauss inclined her head.

"In that case, my lady, allow me to be of service. You require staff—at the least a cook, a butler, and a person of all work. I will contact the agency the firm uses and have them send reliable people. Since it is unlikely that they will arrive before tomorrow morning, I further suggest that I have a meal delivered, so that we may continue our work unimpeded.

"Also, if you will take an old woman's advice—*have* Peers stay with you until the delm returns."

These plans were breathtaking, though surely reasonable, Sinit thought, save—

"Ma'am, I—the former staff was turned off for a reason."

"Perhaps they were, and perhaps we may discover what that reason was. In the meanwhile, if you are concerned about expense, my lady, I can assure you that funds are available. The meal is borne by the firm."

Sinit hesitated. It would be pleasant to have staff, but—

"After all," said Etha dea'Gauss, "*some*one will need to answer the door."

Well, thought Sinit, *that* was certainly true.

She inclined her head.

"Thank you, ma'am. You're very good."

#

Breakfast for Peers and herself was tea and the last biscuits from the last tin in the pantry. She would, Sinit thought, need to go to the market.

The door chimed, interrupting these thoughts. She started to her feet, but Peers was already up and moving.

"Finish your breakfast, my lady. I will answer."

There was no arguing with such authority, Sinit thought, and dunked a stale biscuit in her tea. Peers was back by the time she had disposed of it, and resumed her place at the table.

"Lydberg has answered," the *qe'andra* said composedly, taking up her tea cup.

"But, where is the letter?" Sinit asked.

"At our usual table," Peers answered. "There is no reason that you should be disturbed at your meal by business, my lady."

Sinit picked up her tea cup. She was unused to having such care taken for her; it was both unnerving and comforting. Also –

"I think," she said, meeting Peers's eye, "that I should be Sinit. You have already allowed me Peers, after all." She paused. "I feel that our *melant'is* must be as partners, with I the junior."

Straight eyebrows rose. Peers inclined her head.

"I am honored, Sinit."

She laughed. "Surely, you are! Now, I will tell you that this delightful repast we have just enjoyed is the last food in the pantry. I will go to market today, so that we may—"

"Surely, the cook will do that," Peers interrupted comfortably.

Sinit blinked. "The cook—"

"You will recall that my Aunt Etha had engaged for you three servants from the firm's usual agency. They should be along—"

The door chimed. Peers smiled and rose.

"Very soon," she said. "Shall I bring them to you in the library, or the formal parlor?"

"The library, of your kindness," Sinit said, hastily swallowing the last of her tea. "Thank you, Peers."

#

Lydberg's letter was . . . ungracious. The sum owed was reiterated, with a note that only the signature of Mizel Herself would be acceptable upon the agreement letter, Lydberg having no confidence in the guarantees of *delms-in-waiting*.

"Now, that," Peers said, "is mere spite, my—Sinit. Lydberg surely knows that any letter of agreement must be accepted by the oversight committee. Without that, it matters not who places their name on the line for Mizel."

Sinit tapped the letter. "The sum demanded, as payment for expenses in arrears . . ."

Peers moved her shoulders.

"We found the ledger sheets last evening, did we not? The amounts were paid."

"No," Sinit said, her meager breakfast a stone in her stomach. "I woke in the night realizing, that—it fell to the nadelm to pay the amounts. That does not mean they were paid in fact, though the ledgers tell that tale."

"I was told that the nadelm had been a bad manager," Peers murmured.

"More," Sinit said, swallowing. "He was—expensive, and unfettered. He used Aelliana's quartershare as his own. He only required tribute from Voni, as she brought profit to the clan. For myself—well. I was fourteen when he died, and not yet grown into a quartershare. However, there had been no funds set aside in an account for my majority."

Peers took a careful breath.

"I see. Your theory is, then, that the nadelm . . . failed to pay the sums recorded to Lydberg."

"Most likely, he spent the money on his own pleasure," Sinit said quietly. "My sister Aelliana may know more."

"Then we will make certain to interview her," Peers said.

"In the meanwhile," Sinit said, firmly. "We will settle with Lydberg in good faith."

"If I may," Peers murmured. "We will offer copies of the ledger sheets, and ask Lydberg to show their accounting. This is standard procedure, and so Lydberg's *qe'andra* will instruct the delm. In the meanwhile—"

"In the meanwhile," Sinit interrupted. "We must have a plan in place to pay whatever is truly owed, assuming our ceiling is three cantra. Even should Golindor sell today—"

"That is our other danger," Peers said, interrupting in her turn. "If Lydberg puts it out that Mizel is desperate for cash, we will be seeking to sell at a—greater disadvantage."

Sinit wilted.

"There is another option, my lady," Peers said, after a moment. "Forgive me for noticing that Mizel is thin of adults. Would you be open to buy-ins?"

Sinit stared. "Who would *buy into* Mizel?"

"Well . . ." Peers met her eyes. "Myself, for one."

#

Nuncheon was simple, yet worthy of any meal served to Lady yo'Lanna's table. After, Sinit took herself upstairs. There was no need to open the third floor; there were sufficient bedrooms on the second to accommodate all of Mizel. Merely those that had been shut up ought to be made ready.

Aelliana's former room was stripped to the walls. It was musty, and Sinit crossed to the windows, pushing them open, admitting the sounds of Raingleam Street along with fresh air.

Sinit made a note to explore the storage rooms for furniture—or perhaps Tiatha – for surely this room ought to go to Aelliana's daughter—would like to explore the basements with her aunt Sinit. A shared adventure might ease the awkwardness that must at first stand between them.

The next room was Voni's, which Sinit passed by. The one after had been Ran Eld's.

Sinit pushed the door open, expecting that it had been stripped as bare as Aelliana's—and stood gaping on the threshold.

The room looked as if Ran Eld had left it that morning. The shelves were full of books and ornaments, the floors covered in bright rugs, the wall hung with art, the closet bulging with clothes.

The desk . . . Sinit turned—the desktop was bare; the drawers empty. This, then had been the source of the ledger sheets and sharesbooks they had found on the delm's desk. Suddenly, it made a kind of terrible sense, that Birin Caylon had gone to Low Port, in search of her son, who had all but ruined the clan.

Well.

The room would have to be cleared. It would do for Ver Non, who would no doubt also wish to choose his own furnishings.

Sinit closed the door and went downstairs to fetch Mr. pel'Kosta, her staff of all work.

"This must be made ready for a new occupant, who will wish to choose his own style," she said, opening the door. "What is here must be boxed, labeled, and taken to the storeroom in the cellar. Then the room must be cleaned."

Mr. pel'Kosta neither blanched nor protested, which Sinit felt he had every right to do. Merely he bowed, and stepped into the room, looking about with what seemed a practiced eye.

The door chimed, and Sinit left him to it to go downstairs.

The caller had just been admitted—a slim figure in pilot leathers, pale brown hair pulled away from a beloved face.

"Aelliana!" Sinit flung forward, as if she were no more than a halfling. Her sister caught her in strong arms and they stood for a moment in silent embrace.

"Sinit, I have news. Shall we to the library?"

#

"What is it?" Sinit asked, when the door was shut.

Aelliana stood in the center of the room, her back to Sinit.

"Sister? Is the news—not good?"

Aelliana's shoulders lifted, then fell. She turned, reached into a pocket and held out her hand, fingers curled.

Shivering, Sinit cupped her sister's hand in both of hers.

"Show me."

Slowly, Aelliana unfisted her hand, revealing Mizel's Ring lying in the center of her palm.

Sinit caught her breath.

"Mother—"

"My associate was not in time to save her life. Daav is in Low Port with a Scout team, seeing to everything that is needful."

Sinit took a breath. "Surely, I must . . . go to her. Bring her home."

Aelliana shook her head. "Surely, you must not," she said softly. "My associate sends the Ring with his regrets. He asks me to tell you that he saw what was left of Mizel and that *it's nothing a daughter will want to have as the last memory of her mother.*"

Aelliana sighed. "Clarence is Terran, and has sensibilities. If it eases you, he refused me, also."

Sinit swallowed. "Which is why Daav is seeing to the needful."

"Yes."

The silence stretched. Aelliana extended her hand, Mizel's Ring glittering in her palm.

Biting back tears, Sinit picked the thing up and slipped it onto her finger.

Aelliana moved, sweeping a bow—delm-to-delm—and straightened, face solemn.

"Mizel," she said, her voice strong and sure. "All honor to you."

There came a sharp rap at the door.

Sinit jerked around.

"Come," she said.

Mr. pel'Kosta entered the room, offering a book across both palms.

"My lady, I thought you should see this. I began to box the room abovestairs, as you had requested, and this book fell out of the shelf."

Sinit frowned. It was a novel, which was odd, because Ran Eld had not been bookish. The fall had disarranged the pages, so that they were sticking out beyond—

"Those are stock certificates," Aelliana said sharply, and looked to Sinit. "Whose room?"

"Ran Eld's."

"Of course." Aelliana took a deep breath. "I may be of some assistance, Sister."

"Yes," said Sinit. She looked to Mr. pel'Kosta. "Please ask Ms. dea'Gauss to join us."

"Yes, my lady."

#

"Here."

Aelliana reached to the top shelf and pulled a large bound volume down. She cradled it in one arm and opened the cover, read something and closed it.

"This is the original bound copy of the Caylon revision of the ven'Tura Tables," she said, her voice stringently calm. "I knew he had taken it; I suspected he had burned it, but, no—he would have bragged about that, to make the hurt more poignant."

"Take it," Sinit whispered, and Aelliana nodded absently, already back to scanning the shelves.

"There," she said suddenly. "That blue figurine is Voni's. She wept for a relumma after she *lost* it."

Rapid footsteps came down the hall, and Peers stepped into the room.

"Sinit, what—" She turned her head, and bowed.

"Lady, your pardon."

"No need," Aelliana said, sparing her a bright green glance. "You are Mr. dea'Gauss's granddaughter?"

"I am."

"Then you are the proper person to handle this."

Peers glanced at Sinit.

"This?"

Sinit handed her the book. "It fell off the shelf."

Peers opened it, stared at the crumpled certificates, and took a hard breath.

"This room will have to be thoroughly searched," she said. "My lady, and—my lady, please step out, and leave everything—"

"Aelliana may have that book," Sinit said sharply; "it is hers. We will check it for —inclusions—before she takes it away."

"All else must remain as it is," Peers said. "Lock the door. I will make a call. There is an agency that specializes in this type of room clearing. The firm uses them frequently."

She paused.

"The desk—"

"The desk," Sinit said, hearing the edge in her voice, "was empty before I opened the door."

Peers pressed her lips together, and strode off toward the stairs.

Aelliana stepped into the hallway, and Sinit locked the door.

#

Etha dea'Gauss joined them for a short meeting, staying for prime meal. She left them, promising to send the proper notices to the *Gazette*.

Sinit stood in the hallway, feeling rather wilted.

"May I bring you a glass of wine in the library?" Peers asked.

Sinit looked up.

"Surely it is not your place to serve me."

"Surely, it is my place to offer comfort to my partner after a very long, and absurdly trying day," Peers retorted, and Sinit smiled.

"You are persuasive. Yes. Bring wine for both."

They had scarcely settled when the door chimed, a moment later the butler came to the library.

"Ma'am, Lady Voni pel'Dina Clan Lydberg asks for a word. I am to say she is a friend of your mother."

Peers's eyebrows rose. Sinit took a breath, and placed her glass on the tray before rising.

"Please show Lady Voni in."

#

Voni pel'Dina was small, round, and grey-haired. Her eye fell first on Sinit's face, then on her hand.

Her face tightened.

"Is Birin gone, then?"

"Today," Sinit said, and cleared her throat. "The announcement will be in tomorrow's Gazette."

"You must tell me," the lady said—"by her own hand?"

Sinit stared, leaving Peers to answer.

"She went unguarded to Low Port."

"That is *yes*, then. Lady Caylon—I offer my condolences. I came to offer my services in forming a solution to Lydberg's absurdities, but you are in mourning. I will go. Perhaps you will see me later."

"I think," Sinit said, rather unsteadily, "that we had best see each other now, my lady. Mizel's children must yet be succored."

"Yes," the lady said grimly, and sat in the chair Sinit offered. Peers poured her a glass of wine.

#

"I must ask difficult questions in regard to Mizel's children."

Sinit inclined her head. "Ask."

Lady Voni sighed.

"One has heard that Lydberg received a letter of inquiry from Mizel, on the topic of Mizel's children."

"I think that must be so," Sinit admitted. "I had spoken to my mother regarding my desire to re-clan Mizel's treasures. She was—much in favor, and I believe the delm wrote to Lydberg after we spoke." She took a breath. "There was a letter from Lydberg, in reply."

"Hah." Lady Voni looked sour. "An *invoice* was sent, is what *I* heard."

"A demand, rather," Peers said. "Lydberg states that Mizel is arrears in maintenance payments. Three cantra is required to balance the debt, which would be done by a date, else Lydberg will sell the children's contracts in order to recoup its loss."

"That woman is a fool," Lady Voni said savagely. She had recourse to her glass, and set it aside, empty. Peers rose to refill it.

"One had heard," Sinit murmured, "that Lydberg's Ring has recently passed."

"Indeed it has. The new delm has long been opposed to keeping *non-kin* close. Thus, her first act as delm—ungracious and unsupported by fact. I will tell you how it was."

She took her glass from Peers, sipped, and set it aside.

"Birin was the sister of my heart," Voni pel'Dina said. "When we were children, we swore that, when we had each fulfilled our duties to our clans, we would live together forever."

She sipped her wine, lowered the glass, and met Sinit's eyes.

"When Mizel's finances became complicated, Birin came to me. Between us, we agreed that the best course was to foster the grandchildren to me, and so it was done. It was to only have been a year or two, that it went longer made no matter. I cared for Birin's children as if they were my own – indeed, my heart insists that they *are* my own! They were raised with Lydberg's children, but it was I who gladly bore the expense of their support, their education, their pleasures. My brother, Lydberg-who-was, granted them space in the clanhouse—there was no reason not to do so, we have room for more than we are, even now."

She sent Sinit a sharp look.

"You want them, you said. Why?"

"They are Mizel's treasures," Sinit said. "It has—long troubled me, that they were kept apart from us, though it may have been for the best. One's elder brother—"

The lady raised her hand. "Speak no more of your elder brother. I understand what you would say. Birin knew, I think, but she would hear nothing against him. It was your elder brother drove us apart, and I daresay it was your elder brother who drove her to her death!"

She raised her glass.

"If I may ask, your ladyship?" Peers said.

"Whatever you must, *Qe'andra*. I would see this solved properly."

"You testify that you supported the children. We have journals detailing payments made to Lydberg, for maintenance."

"Birin had made some representation that Mizel ought to pay a stipend, but I put her aside. There was no need."

"And yet . . ."

Her ladyship sighed sharply. "Yes, *Qe'andra—and yet*. May I suppose it was the boy who recorded those payments to Lydberg?"

"In fact."

"Then there you have it," she said. "Whatever those amounts were, they went directly into his pocket."

She turned back to Sinit.

"I regret that I must ask another hard question, lady. Do you *know* the children?"

Sinit sighed.

"To my sorrow, I do not. I wish to rectify that."

"I see that you do." She lapsed into silence, sipping her wine, and looking at some point beyond the bookshelves.

Sinit looked to Peers. Peers raised an eyebrow.

Lady Voni spoke.

"I believe we may assist each other," she said slowly. "I will provide a full accounting of my financial support of Mizel's treasures to the *qe'andra* of Mizel and Lydberg. I will further provide a statement that there is no repayment necessary. Mind you, Lydberg may still demand room and board, but I believe that amount will be found to lie *well* below three cantra."

"If you allow, Lady Caylon, after the House has mourned, I will come again, and talk to you of the children."

"I would be grateful," Sinit said, and her ladyship smiled.

"It will be my very great pleasure. In the meanwhile, I will put one more thing before you and then decently take my leave. It is in my mind that it were best if I found another House to shelter me. Though Birin is gone, I would honor her by coming into Mizel."

Sinit blinked. Lady Voni raised her hand.

"There are many things to consider. I am employed as a traffic controller at Chonselta Spaceport; that income would of course come to Mizel. I have been accustomed to assisting the delm in administrative matters. That experience would of course be placed at Mizel's service.

"However, you may not wish to have the foster-mother with the children. There could be repercussions, given existing alliances, and the fact that I am many years your elder, and have raised for you a brilliant and strong-willed foursome."

"Good," Sinit said, and her ladyship laughed.

"Excellent! We will talk again, soon." She rose, and Sinit with her.

"Thank you," she said. "I am very glad you came."

"As I am, Lady Caylon. As I am."

#

Voni Caylon came home for the twelve days of mourning, returning to her employment on the morning of the thirteenth day, taking most of her things with her.

Sinit was confirmed as Mizel before the Council of Clans.

The *qe'andra* for Clans Mizel and Lydberg settled upon a figure due Lydberg to cover room and board for four fosterlings. The sum was paid from the proceeds of the sale of Golindor Manufacturing.

Voni pel'Dina was provisionally admitted to Clan Mizel, pending a review at the end of six years.

Korval's payment for a scholar-expert, due when Sinit became delm, had been deposited to Mizel's account.

The financial papers found in Ran Eld's room were under examination by the Accountants Guild.

Bedrooms had been made ready for the return of Mizel's treasures.

Mr. orn'Verz, the cook, was preparing a feast, and the children—

The children were due very soon now, with their foster-mother.

Sinit sat in her favorite chair in the library. Mizel's Ring glowed on her hand, the motto bright: *From every storm, a rainbow.*

A familiar step sounded and she turned to smile at Peers.

"You were right," she said. "Mizel *can* afford you."

Peers smiled. "Did I not say that I was a realist? But I wonder—"

"What do you wonder, my friend?"

"I wonder if you have thought any further about allowing me to buy in to Mizel. Your membership is still thin of adults, and I would be an asset to the House."

"Peers, you cannot be serious."

"But I am! My clan has my heir, and I am inconvenient to clan administration, even as I am valued for my gifts. My grandfather has spoken to me several times about the notion of starting my own business, but that does not solve the clan, which surely does *not* need two delms. As a member of Mizel, I would support the delm, and bring the House a trade."

"A trade?"

"Certainly! You have completed your coursework. How if we set up as *qe'andra* at hire, serving those clans who cannot afford the larger firms? We would maintain our ties with the firm, and I daresay some elders like my aunt Etha would be eager to help out occasionally—" She grinned—"for a fee."

Sinit laughed. "You have thought this through, I see."

"I have. Please, my lady. Have me."

Sinit looked up at the woman who had become her very dear friend, and extended a hand. Peers caught it between both of hers.

"Let us meet tomorrow at our usual table and discuss this in depth," Sinit said. "For the moment, I am—interested."

Peers's eyes glowed.

"Then we are half-way to an accord, my lady."

The door chimed.

"That will be the children," Sinit said, rising, and shaking out her dress. She took a breath to steady her nerves.

Peers bowed. "Mizel."

The absurd gesture gave her heart, and she swept out of the library with her head high and a smile on her face, to welcome Mizel's treasures home.

Authors' Afterword

Back, back, a long way back, it was the proud tradition of anthologies not to accept stories written in existing universes. The reasons given were several: (1) that a story set in an on-going enterprise would not be accessible to readers unfamiliar with the property, and (2) that stories written in one setting would of necessity be . . . all the same sort of story. Which is to say boring. Anthology editors as a breed are against inaccessible boring stories, and who can blame them?

However! We here at the Liaden Universe® have long thought that these editorial assumptions were – not well thought out. We believe that a writer of sufficient skill—which is to say most working writers of our acquaintance—are perfectly able to make any story they undertake to tell accessible to readers—that being exactly what writers *do*—and that an established, on-going setting does not by any means equate to a *static* setting. In fact, the opposite. A story grown in a well-thought-out, well-loved, and familiar setting gains weight and credibility.

The Liaden Universe®, for instance, encompasses—well. A universe. It has history. It has people. Of different races, cultures, and necessity. We have written romances set in the Liaden Universe®. We have written mysteries set in the Liaden Universe®. We have written westerns set in the Liaden Universe®. We've mixed it all up, down and sideways.

The Liaden Universe® now encompasses more than 80 works—and it's still expanding.

The three stories included in this chapbook take place in the Liaden Universe®. Each deals with the aftermath of a great upheaval, or storm. Each story is different, and we trust and believe that they are all accessible.

"Standing Orders" was written for theme anthology *Derelict*, edited by David B. Coe and Joshua Palmatier. For it, we went 'way back into Liaden Universe® history, to the time of the AI Wars, to talk about betrayal, what it means to be a person, and how the heroes in life are very often those you never see celebrated.

"From Every Storm a Rainbow" was written for Baen.com, to fulfill an editorial desire for a "holiday" feel. For this story of a family reforged we went to Liad itself, and more recent history—following the sister of mainline character Aelliana Caylon as she reclaims the treasures of her House.

And then there is "Songs of the Fathers," featuring Lomar Fasholt.

A valued associate of mainline character Shan yos'Galan, Lomar was first introduced in *Conflict of Honors*, 33 "real world" years ago. She has been missing for quite a while, even in story time. We tried several times to fit her story into recent novels, but it never worked. One attempt will-or-has-been serialized to Splinter Universe—that was the attempt that wanted to be its own novel, but again – there was no room in either our planning or our contracts for a Lomar novel.

For Lomar's story, we went to yet another part of the Liaden Universe® to explore what happens when faith becomes dogma and the consciences of good people are abused.

So! Three stories, all set in the existing Liaden Universe®, in whose spacelanes we the authors have been laboring for nearly 40 years, each one as different from the other as they might be. They make, so we think, an interesting set, and we hope you enjoyed reading them as much as we enjoyed writing them.

Sharon Lee and Steve Miller
Cat Farm and Confusion Factory
October 2022

About the Authors

Co-authors Sharon Lee and Steve Miller have been working in the fertile fields of genre fiction for more than thirty years, pioneering today's sub-genre of science fiction romance–stories that contain all the action, adventure and sense of wonder of traditional space opera, with the addition of romantic relationships.

Over the course of their partnership, Lee and Miller have written thirty-four novels, twenty-five in their long-running, original space opera setting, the Liaden Universe®, where honor, wit, and true love are potent weapons against deceit and treachery.

There are more than 300,000 Liaden Universe® novels in print. Liaden titles regularly place in the top ten bestsellers in *Locus Magazine*, the trade paper of the speculative fiction genres. Twelve Lee and Miller titles have been national bestsellers.

Liaden Universe® novels have twice won the Prism Award for Best Futuristic Romance, reader and editor choice awards from *Romantic Times*, as well as the Hal Clement Award for Best YA Science Fiction Novel, proving the appeal of the series to a wide range of readers.

Lee and Miller's work in the field has not been limited to writing fiction.

Sharon Lee served three years as the first full-time executive director of the Science Fiction and Fantasy Writers of America, and went on to be elected vice-president, and president of that organization. She has been a Nebula Award jurist.

Steve Miller was the founding curator of the University of Maryland's Science Fiction Research Collection. He has been a jurist for the Philip K. Dick Award.

Lee and Miller have together appeared at science fiction conventions around the country, as writer guests of honor and principal speakers. They have been panelists, participated in writing workshops, and given talks on subjects as diverse as proper curating of a cat whisker collection, techniques for creating believable characters, and world-building alien societies.

In 2012, Lee and Miller were jointly awarded the E.E. "Doc" Smith Memorial Award for Imaginative Fiction (a.k.a. the "Skylark" Award), given annually by the New England Science Fiction Association to someone who has contributed significantly to science fiction, both through work in the field and by exemplifying the personal qualities which made the late "Doc" Smith well-loved by those who knew him. Previous recipients include George R.R. Martin, Anne McCaffrey, and Sir Terry Pratchett.

Sharon Lee and Steve Miller met in a college writing course in 1978; they married in 1980. In 1988, they moved from their native Maryland to Maine, where they may still be found, in a sun-filled house in a small Central Maine town. Their household currently includes four Maine coon cats.

Steve and Sharon maintain a web presence at korval.com

Novels by Sharon Lee & Steve Miller

The Liaden Universe®: *Agent of Change* * *Conflict of Honors* * *Carpe Diem* * *Plan B* * *Local Custom* * *Scout's Progress* * *I Dare* * *Balance of Trade* * *Crystal Soldier* * *Crystal Dragon* * *Fledgling* * *Saltation* * *Mouse and Dragon* * *Ghost Ship* * *Dragon Ship* * *Necessity's Child* * *Trade Secret* * *Dragon in Exile* * *Alliance of Equals* * *The Gathering Edge* * *Neogenesis* * *Accepting the Lance* * *Trader's Leap* * *Fair Trade* * *Salvage Right*

Omnibus Editions: *The Dragon Variation* * *The Agent Gambit* * *Korval's Game* * *The Crystal Variation*

Story Collections: *A Liaden Universe Constellation: Volume 1* * *A Liaden Universe Constellation: Volume 2* * *A Liaden Universe Constellation: Volume 3* * *A Liaden Universe Constellation: Volume 4* * *A Liaden Universe Constellation: Volume 5*

The Fey Duology: *Duainfey* * *Longeye*

Gem ser'Edreth: *The Tomorrow Log*

Novels by Sharon Lee

The Carousel Trilogy: *Carousel Tides* * *Carousel Sun* * *Carousel Seas*

Jennifer Pierce Maine Mysteries: *Barnburner* * *Gunshy*

Pinbeam Books Publications

Sharon Lee and Steve Miller's indie publishing arm

Adventures in the Liaden Universe®: *Two Tales of Korval* * *Fellow Travelers* * *Duty Bound* * *Certain Symmetry* * *Trading in Futures* * *Changeling* * *Loose Cannon* * *Shadows and Shades* * *Quiet Knives* * *With Stars Underfoot* * *Necessary Evils* * *Allies* * *Dragon Tide* * *Eidolon* * *Misfits* * *Halfling Moon* **Skyblaze* * *Courier Run* * *Legacy Systems* * *Moon's Honor* * *Technical Details* * *Sleeping with the Enemy* * *Change Management* * *Due Diligence* * *Cultivar* * *Heirs to Trouble* * *Degrees of Separation* * *Fortune's Favor* * *Shout of Honor* * *The Gate that Locks the Tree* * *Ambient Conditions* * *Change State* * *Bad Actors* * *Bread Alone* * *From Every Storm*

Splinter Universe Presents: *Splinter Universe Presents: Volume One* * *The Wrong Lance*

By Sharon Lee: *Variations Three* * *Endeavors of Will* * *The Day they Brought the Bears to Belfast* * *Surfside* * *The Gift of Magic* * *Spell Bound* * *Writing Neep*

By Steve Miller: *Chariot to the Stars* * *TimeRags II*

By Sharon Lee and Steve Miller: *Calamity's Child* * *The Cat's Job* * *Master Walk* * *Quiet Magic* * *The Naming of Kinzel* * *Reflections on Tinsori Light*

THANK YOU

Thank you for your support of our work.
Sharon Lee and Steve Miller

Made in the USA
Las Vegas, NV
10 March 2024